DYING
BREATH

DYING BREATH

M A COMLEY

2018

New York Times and USA Today bestselling author M A Comley
Published by Jeamel Publishing limited
Copyright © 2018 M A Comley
Digital Edition, License Notes

This is a work of fiction. Names, characters, places and incidents are a product of the author's imagination or are used fictitiously, and any resemblance to actual persons living or dead, business establishments, events or locales is entirely coincidental.

ISBN-13: 978-1724388063

ISBN-10: 1724388061

OTHER BOOKS BY M A COMLEY

Blind Justice (Novella)

Cruel Justice (Book #1)

Mortal Justice (Novella)

Impeding Justice (Book #2)

Final Justice (Book #3)

Foul Justice (Book #4)

Guaranteed Justice (Book #5)

Ultimate Justice (Book #6)

Virtual Justice (Book #7)

Hostile Justice (Book #8)

Tortured Justice (Book #9)

Rough Justice (Book #10)

Dubious Justice (Book #11)

Calculated Justice (Book #12)

Twisted Justice (Book #13)

Justice at Christmas (Short Story)

Prime Justice (Book #14)

Heroic Justice (Book #15)

Shameful Justice (Book #16)

Immoral Justice (Book #17)

Unfair Justice (a 10,000 word short story)

Irrational Justice (a 10,000 word short story)

Seeking Justice (a 15,000 word novella)

Clever Deception (co-written by Linda S Prather)

Tragic Deception (co-written by Linda S Prather)

Sinful Deception (co-written by Linda S Prather)

Forever Watching You (DI Miranda Carr thriller)

Wrong Place (DI Sally Parker thriller #1)

No Hiding Place (DI Sally Parker thriller #2)

Cold Case (DI Sally Parker thriller#3)

Deadly Encounter (DI Sally Parker thriller #4)

Lost Innocence (DI Sally Parker thriller #5)

Web of Deceit (DI Sally Parker Novella with Tara Lyons)

The Missing Children (DI Kayli Bright #1)

Killer On The Run (DI Kayli Bright #2)

Hidden Agenda (DI Kayli Bright #3)

Murderous Betrayal (Kayli Bright #4)

Dying Breath (Kayli Bright #5)

The Caller (co-written with Tara Lyons)

Evil In Disguise – a novel based on True events

Deadly Act (Hero series novella)

Torn Apart (Hero series #1)

End Result (Hero series #2)

In Plain Sight (Hero Series #3)

Double Jeopardy (Hero Series #4)

Sole Intention (Intention series #1)

Grave Intention (Intention series #2)

Devious Intention (Intention #3)

Merry Widow (A Lorne Simpkins short story)

It's A Dog's Life (A Lorne Simpkins short story)

A Time To Heal (A Sweet Romance)

A Time For Change (A Sweet Romance)

High Spirits

The Temptation series (Romantic Suspense/New Adult Novellas)

Past Temptation

Lost Temptation

KEEP IN TOUCH WITH THE AUTHOR:

Twitter
https://twitter.com/Melcom1

Blog
http://melcomley.blogspot.com

Facebook
http://smarturl.it/sps7jh

Newsletter
http://smarturl.it/8jtcvv

BookBub
www.bookbub.com/authors/m-a-comley

ACKNOWLEDGMENTS

This book is dedicated to the one person who has stood by me through thick and thin throughout my life, my beautiful Mother, Jean.

Thank you to Kayli and Donna from my ARC group for allowing me to use their names in this series.

My thanks as always go to my talented editor Stefanie Spangler Buswell and to Karri Klawiter for her cover design expertise.

My heartfelt thanks as always go to my wonderful proofreader, Emmy Ellis for spotting all the lingering nits. I'd be lost without you.

PROLOGUE

"Mum, I need money to pay for the rest of the trip today. You asked me to remind you."

Jessica sighed and picked up her purse off the kitchen table. She opened the flap and shook her head. "A little notice would have been nice, Cathy. I haven't got any cash in my purse."

"Sorry. Want me to nip down to the hole in the wall for you?"

Jessica mulled the idea over for a few moments before deciding against it. "No, I'll do it."

"That's nuts. You're not even dressed yet. You know it takes you an eternity to get ready in the morning. Give me your card. It's not as if I haven't done it for you in the past."

"You can be such an impatient minx at times. Okay, the number is—"

"Six eight three seven. Yeah, it's imprinted on my mind," Cathy said with a chuckle.

"Is that so? Maybe I should consider changing my PIN if that's the case."

"Whatever. Don't you trust me, Mum? I wouldn't dream of nicking any of your money without your say so."

She leaned over and ran a hand down her daughter's cheek. "I know you wouldn't, darling. I was jesting. I trust you with my life. Go on then—get out what you need for your trip and take an extra tenner for yourself."

"What about topping up your purse?"

"You're right. Get me out an extra twenty then, but no more."

Her sixteen-year-old daughter smiled, snatched the card from her hand, and sprinted out the back door. Jessica took the time alone to reflect on how lucky she was to have such a loving family around her when most of her friends were 'happily single' again after their divorces, except they weren't. Though the cracks in their joyful charades were easy to see, she would never dream of tackling them about the lies they were telling, for fear of hurting their feelings.

She sighed contentedly as her husband's handsome features filled her mind. He was away for a few days, some kind of trade fair to do with his business, not that she was that interested in his business, as long as it brought in the money to keep the substantial roof over her head and paid the gardener every month to care for the five acres they owned.

The house was newly built, and they'd lived there for only a month. She was eager to get the paddocks in good shape before she transferred her beautiful stallion, Nutmeg, to his new home. His stable had been erected, but she was far from satisfied that the paddock was free from all the nails and debris left behind after the construction. The more she'd instructed the builders to clean up after themselves, the more they'd seemed to ignore her pleas, so much that she'd delayed Nutmeg's arrival.

Once Cathy was out of her hair and at school, Jessica intended to spend the day with her beautiful Nutmeg. She had neglected him lately because of the move and all it entailed. She was one of those women who worked her socks off to make sure her new home was up and running promptly. After three days of hard work, not a single packing box remained in sight, and the house looked warm and inviting, as if it had been their family home for years instead of mere days.

She had spent weeks planning out the garden with the landscapers and the build team, ensuring that Nutmeg would be moving into a beautiful home with enough space to trot around in. But no one could have foreseen the dreadful downpours they would have to contend with throughout the month of May.

Panting from her exertion, Cathy entered the back door and placed her mother's card and money on the kitchen table. "One hundred and fifty for the trip, a tenner for me and twenty for you, and there's the ticket to prove I haven't pinched anything else."

Jessica frowned. "I believe you, love. Why would you say that?" She placed a concerned hand over her daughter's.

"No reason, Mum. I just don't like you thinking that I take advantage of you. Look, I better get off to school now. Have a fun day with Nutmeg. Give him a hug from me." Cathy pecked her mother on the cheek, picked up her school bag, and left the house.

Jessica placed her card and money in her purse, locked the back door, and went upstairs to get ready for her trip to the stables.

Almost forty minutes later, she left the house, her hair still damp from her shower, and immediately got ensnared in the traffic. She lashed out at the steering wheel of her four-wheel drive. "Why didn't I leave it an extra ten minutes? What the heck was I thinking?" Her eagerness had far outweighed any common sense she'd owned when she'd set off.

She turned on upbeat music to distract her and to attempt to keep her calm during the traffic jam. It worked, too—another twenty minutes dragged by until she pulled into the livery yard a few miles from her home. She spotted Belinda Moss coming out of a nearby stable and ignored her. Belinda turned her head swiftly, obviously embarrassed, and made her way into the next stall to tend to someone else's horse.

As long as she keeps her distance, everything should be fine. I'll ignore her. I have a handsome stallion waiting for me.

She pulled the bag of carrots she'd bought the day before out of the boot and lugged it over to Nutmeg's stable. He was pretty vocal when he saw her walking towards him. "Hello, beautiful. How are you today?"

He neighed and nodded, his ears twitching at the sound of her voice. Jessica opened the stable door and stepped in. She lugged the sack of carrots through the stable to the small room out the back, where she kept all of Nutmeg's accessories in what amounted to a mini tack room. She laughed when her horse followed her and nudged her in the back continuously until she relented to his charms and gave him a carrot or three.

She ran her hand down the length of his nose. "Have you missed me, boy?"

Nutmeg was too busy munching on his carrot to respond. She was lucky, though. He was a super-intelligent horse and understood ninety percent of what she said. Obviously, she occasionally ranted and raved about things—such as the incident that had taken place at the stables recently—and he looked at her a little non-plussed. Overall, though, they had a wonderful relationship that had been built on trust and compassion since Nutmeg had come into her life as a foal over five years ago.

Her anger mounted as the incident reared its ugly head yet again in her mind. "It's over with now. I need to move on. We need to move on. Don't we, mate?" Nutmeg finished chewing his carrot and neighed, nodding adamantly in response to her question. She kissed his nose. "What would I do without you to keep me sane, when all of those around me appear to be losing their heads?"

Nutmeg nodded again and pawed at the ground impatiently with his front hoof. "All right, I get the hint. I'm as desperate as you are to get a ride in this morning before the rain descends upon us this afternoon."

She gathered his saddle and bridle from the tack room and placed them gently on Nutmeg. She always treated her horse with kid gloves. She cared about him, which was why her blood had boiled when she'd learnt what had happened with Belinda. *Focus! Ignore what she did. She's not worth it. Anger eats away at you like an unforgiving cancer. Ignore and move on.*

Once Nutmeg was fitted with his equipment, Jessica removed her riding hat from the shelf and placed it securely on her head, attaching the strap under her chin, before she led Nutmeg out of the stable and into the courtyard.

Another regular, Melissa Cartwright, stopped to talk to her briefly as her horse, Daisy, nuzzled Nutmeg affectionately. "Hey, maybe we should consider mating them one day," Melissa joked.

Jessica shrugged. "I'm up for it, if you are. They seem to get on well, and any foals they had would no doubt have beautiful markings and a temperament to match."

"Let's arrange that soon then. We could go halves on what we get for their offspring."

Jessica inhaled a large breath then shook her head. "I doubt if I'd be able to part with the foal. Could you? In all honesty?"

Melissa's mouth turned down at the sides. "Now that you've said it, not sure I could. Maybe that was a bad idea to even suggest it."

"No, it was a fabulous idea, but the outcome needs careful consideration before we embark on the adventure. I'm sure these two would be up for it anyway—they're such flirts."

They both laughed and went their separate ways. Jessica loved to exercise Nutmeg in the nearby forest before she let him gallop through the open fields beyond. She led him towards the entrance, walking at his side, enjoying the stroll.

When she mounted him, he fidgeted until she was settled in one position. That was unusual for him. They set off, picking their way through the forest. Jessica had to duck beneath the branches, which were bending more than usual because of the constant rain over the last few weeks. Once they were into a wide open clearing, she encouraged Nutmeg to trot a little. He did so willingly, and the wind in her hair in the woodland felt good. A few hundred yards ahead of them, a large fallen tree blocked the path. Jessica mentally prepared herself for the jump. She'd only jumped a few objects with Nutmeg over the years and didn't want to put extra strain on his joints. They'd never jumped anything as huge as the tree trunk.

She patted his neck. "We can do this, big boy. Dig deep and give me all you've got."

Nutmeg neighed and upped his pace slightly. She had every confidence in his ability to jump over the trunk, but a few feet from it, Nutmeg began to fidget. His pace slowed then sped up, which Jessica thought strange. She considered dismounting to walk him around the offending object, but at the last minute, she decided against it, dug him hard with her heel, and shouted, encouraging him to glide over the trunk.

Nutmeg did her proud by flying over it, but once he landed on the other side, something spooked him, and he reared up. Unprepared for the sudden movement, Jessica let go of the reins and fell backwards. The impact on her spine took her breath away. The last thing she heard before she drifted into unconsciousness was the sound of Nutmeg galloping away from her...

CHAPTER ONE

Belinda heard the commotion and looked up from mucking out one of the stables to find Nutmeg rearing up in the courtyard. *What the heck! Why doesn't Jessica keep that damn horse under control?*

She stormed out of the stable towards him, only to realise he no longer had his saddle on and that Jessica was nowhere to be seen.

Susan Lord, the livery owner, came running out of the office across from the stables. "What's going on here?" she demanded.

"Hey, don't blame me for this. The last time I saw Jessica she was riding off with him."

Susan twisted around, searching for Jessica. "Where is she?"

Belinda shrugged. "I haven't got a clue. I was mucking out when Nutmeg ran into the yard and started causing a disturbance."

"Okay, now I'm worried. Jess would never leave him. How long has it been since you saw her last?"

"About twenty minutes, give or take. What? You think something has happened to her?"

"Don't you? Where's his damn saddle, for starters. Get everyone together—we need to initiate a search. I think something serious has happened to her. God, I hope I'm wrong about that."

Belinda sprang into action, rounding up everyone she could find. Minutes later, six anxious people were standing in the yard, awaiting instructions.

Susan took control of the situation. "Does anyone know what route Jessica usually takes?"

"It depends what mood she's in. Sometimes she goes through the paddocks and across the fields, or other times, she might go through the forest," Belinda said.

Susan looked over at Nutmeg, who had been secured by a rope to a hook on the wall outside his stable. She approached the stallion and ran her hand down his front leg. "He's not wet. I don't think he could have gone over the fields." She lifted his hoof, and Belinda spotted the telltale remnants of leaves and bark around his shoe. "Okay, my detection skills might be way off here, but I'm willing to take a bet that she went through the woods. We need to get out there and see what's going on. Those with available horses, saddled up, ready to ride, I suggest you head off first. The rest of us will join you as soon as we're able to."

"It won't take me a second to saddle up Shadow," Belinda announced.

Susan nodded. "You can lead the way, Belinda. Make it snappy. My concern levels are rising the longer she's missing."

Belinda ran into the stable, patted her black stallion on the neck, and hurriedly placed the saddle on his back. "Come on, boy. We've got a job to do." The pair of them emerged from the stable within minutes. Belinda got on her horse and waited as the others setting off with her all mounted their rides. Once everyone was ready, Belinda set off at a fast trot, the rest of the group not far behind her.

"Good luck. Let me know what you find," Susan shouted.

"We will." Belinda patted her jacket pocket to check she was carrying her phone.

It took the group ten minutes to reach the forest. They hadn't travelled far when Belinda spotted something red ahead of her. "Damn, looks like we found her. Come on, quickly."

The four riders upped their pace and came to a standstill alongside Jessica's body, her saddle lying close by.

Belinda was the first to dismount. She raced over to Jessica. "Jess, oh my God! Jess, are you all right?" She shook Jessica a little until one of the other women in the group advised her not to touch her.

"Leave her be, Belinda. There's no telling what damage has been done. I'll call for an ambulance," Maureen said.

Belinda sat back on her heels and stared at Jessica. She was unconscious, her body twisted at an awkward angle over the tree trunk. She could see from the rise and fall of Jess's chest that she was alive but that her breathing was erratic. She figured that was due to the fall Jessica had likely had. "Will someone ring Susan, tell her we've found Jessica?"

"I'll do it," Paula said, fishing out her phone from the bumbag she was wearing.

"Jess, can you hear me?" Belinda asked, bending closer. "I'm sorry. I didn't mean to…"

19

Maureen stood at Jessica's head. "The ambulance is on its way. Should be here in around ten minutes."

"I hope they get here sooner, her breathing has become far more irregular since we found her," Belinda said, glancing up at the older woman.

"What do you think happened?"

Belinda surveyed the scene. "My guess is Nutmeg jumped the trunk then probably stood on something and reared up, tipping Jess off."

"That's all well and good, but what about her saddle? That should have remained in place, surely?"

Belinda nodded. "Perhaps Jess didn't fasten it properly and it came loose in the fall."

"Hard to believe with Jess. She's an experienced rider, after all," Maureen replied with a frown pulling at her brow.

Belinda threw her arms up in the air. "I don't know. I'm just surmising. I'll take a peep in my crystal ball if you like."

"Whoa! Don't get on your high horse with me. It was a simple suggestion. Maybe I'll keep my theories to myself in the future."

"Sorry. I didn't mean to snap. I'm concerned."

"Aren't we all?" Maureen backed away from Belinda, giving her a scathing look.

Ten minutes dragged by until finally, in the distance, the wail of the siren approached.

"I'll go back to the opening and guide them through," Maureen offered before setting off at a brisk pace.

Belinda ran a gentle hand down Jess's face. "Come on, wake up, Jess. Don't leave us."

"Don't talk like that, Belinda. She's not going anywhere. She'll pull through this, I'm sure," Paula said.

"I hope you're right. However, I think since we showed up, she's deteriorated."

The rustle behind them signified the arrival of the two paramedics, the first an older male and the second a young female.

"Step aside if you will, miss," the man ordered.

Belinda stood and took a few steps back. She watched as the paramedics checked Jess's vital signs and assessed her injuries.

"We need the back board. I'm assuming her back is broken," the male paramedic said.

Everyone gathered gasped when they heard the news. Belinda shook her head. *How dreadful, poor Jess. I hope the paramedic is wrong.*

"Did any of you ladies see what happened? Was anyone with her?"

Belinda acted as spokesperson for the group. "No, she was out riding alone. Her horse came back to the yard, and we went out to find her immediately. We found her like this just before we rang you. Her breathing has got a lot worse since we discovered her. Can you help her? She's not going to die, is she?"

"That's extremely difficult to say at present. We'll get her on a stretcher and back to the hospital as quickly as we can. It'll be up to the doctors to try and do all they can to save her."

"Shouldn't a doctor be here? To evaluate her before she's moved? Aren't you at risk of causing more damage to her if you move her as she is?"

"Ordinarily, I would agree with you, but I fear there isn't time to hang around waiting for the doctor to come. If the person who placed the call had indicated the likelihood of her having a broken back, then maybe a mobile doctor could have attended the scene."

"I'm sorry. There was no way I could have known that when I rang 999," Maureen stated.

"Sorry, I wasn't casting aspersions. It's just that the more information we are given at the time the better we can make an assessment of the patient's needs going forward. You rang us, and that's enough to get the ball rolling."

Maureen nodded, appearing to be at a loss for anything else to say.

The female paramedic arrived with the back board and positioned it on the ground beside Jessica. The two paramedics lifted Jessica carefully onto the board. Then they carried her to the ambulance and set off towards the hospital while the women collected their horses and returned to the stables, fear and concern for Jessica steering their every move.

Susan was waiting anxiously in the middle of the yard when they arrived. "Well, what's going on?"

Belinda sighed heavily. "They've taken her to hospital with a suspected broken back."

Susan covered her face with her hands and shook her head. "No. Not Jessica. She's such a safe rider—how the bloody hell could something like this happen?"

"It's no good asking that now. What's done is done. We need to keep her in our thoughts and pray that she comes through this. Her family should be told."

"Oh gosh, you're right. I'll look up her husband's number now. I think he's down as her next of kin." Susan rushed into the office while Belinda stabled Shadow, removed his saddle, then joined Susan in the office.

"He's away at the moment. I managed to get in touch with him, and he told me he's got a meeting to attend to before he can return home."

Belinda frowned. "That's odd. I thought he'd be here like a shot. I know I would be if my other half was in danger."

"He's up in Liverpool. It's going to take him a couple of hours to get here. He told me to ring her daughter's school. Make sure Cathy was aware her mother is in hospital."

"Really? Would you?" Belinda asked, shocked by the decision.

Susan seemed confused. "I'm not sure I would, but it's what he wants. Maybe they have some sort of code they adhere to in case something like this ever takes place."

"I don't like it. You don't put that kind of pressure on a young girl's shoulders. I'd be more inclined to ring Jess's parents than her daughter, if I were in your shoes."

"You're right. Damn, I hope Wesley doesn't take umbrage when he finds out I've gone against his wishes."

"That's tough. He should have thought about ringing Jess's parents himself. Maybe they've fallen out? Who knows? That's the best way to proceed in my opinion, Susan."

"I think you're right. Christ, what was Jess's maiden name? My head is all over the place right now."

"Watson. I remember Jessica recently introducing her sister Amelia to us."

Susan clicked her fingers and pointed at Belinda. "You're right—she did. Maybe it would be better if I rang her sister instead of her parents. What do you think?"

"It doesn't really matter. We're wasting time. I think she lives in the Abbots Leigh area. I'll look her number up on the internet." Belinda found Amelia's number within seconds and called it. Her home number rang for a while before it was answered. "Amelia?"

"That's right. You've come through to my mobile. Who is this?"

"It's Belinda Moss, down at Hawthorn Stables. Not sure if you remember me or not?"

"I do. What can I do for you, Belinda?"

She inhaled a large breath then let it out slowly before she spoke again. "I'm afraid I have some bad news for you regarding your sister, Jessica."

"What? Bad news? Tell me?"

"It looks like she fell off Nutmeg this morning in the forest. We found her as soon as we could, and the paramedics have taken her to the hospital."

"What? No! Is she all right?"

"I'm sorry. I think you should know from the outset that the paramedics thought Jess had broken her back in the fall."

"No! Oh my God. What about Wesley? Has anyone rung him?"

"Yes, he's in Liverpool at a meeting he can't get out of apparently. He wanted us to ring Cathy, but I thought that was a bit much and tracked down your number. I hope I've done the right thing?"

"You have. Thank goodness you didn't ring Cathy. What was he thinking? I'll call the rest of the family, and we'll get over to the hospital as soon as we can. Thanks for ringing me. I really appreciate it."

~ ~ ~

Amelia rang her parents and arranged to drop by and pick them up twenty minutes later. Together, they drove to the hospital in stunned silence.

Amelia approached the young lady on reception and said, "Hi, we're Jessica Porter's family—sister, mother, and father. Is it all right if we see her?"

"Let me check our records. Ah, yes, the doctor is in with her now, assessing her injuries. I'll get someone to show you through to the family room and inform the doctor that you're here."

"Thank you." Amelia stepped away from the desk to join her parents. She clung to her mother's hand tightly until a male nurse arrived to speak to them.

"Hi, if you'd like to follow me." He led them up the hallway and around the corner into a large family room that had a child's play area off to one side. On the other there were seats placed along the length of the wall. "The doctor should be with you soon. Try not to worry too much."

The three of them sat down.

However it wasn't long before Amelia's father stood up again and paced the room. "How could this happen? Jessica has always been extra cautious when she's been out riding."

"Now, Gerald, until we know all the facts, we can't be sure what Jessica failed to do to ensure her safety. What I do know is that our daughter is now in hospital, fighting for her life." Mary Watson broke down and cried.

Amelia placed an arm around her mother's shoulders and pulled her in tight. "There's no use speculating until we know all the facts. I'm going to try and ring Wesley. He should be here." She stepped out of the room and rang her brother-in-law's mobile number. It went into voicemail after the second ring. "Wesley, we're at the Bristol Royal Infirmary. We've yet to see the doctor about how bad Jessica is, but we sure could do with you being here. Please come as soon as you can." She hung up and trudged back to the family room on heavy legs. "What shall we do about Cathy?"

Her mother looked up as fresh tears swam in her eyes. "Someone should be there when she gets home from school. We've got a few hours before then. Hopefully, we'll find out what's going on soon then we can decide what to do for the best. Did you get through to Wes?"

"No. I left a message on his voicemail." Amelia sat next to her mother again.

"He should be here," her father said angrily.

"He's away on business, Dad. He couldn't have known anything of this nature was going to happen. I'm sure he'll get here as soon as he can."

"We'll see. I know if any of you lot had an accident, wild horses couldn't keep me away. Oh no, did I really utter those words? Was that damned horse all right?"

Amelia nodded. "As far as I know. He returned to the stable to alert them. The search began instantly. He's a clever horse. Don't blame him for this, Dad."

Her father flung a hand in the air and grunted his disapproval. Amelia gripped her mother's hand for support, and the room fell silent.

Around ten minutes later, a middle-aged doctor with thinning hair and spectacles walked into the room. "Hello there. Are you Jessica Porter's family?"

Amelia and her mother stood.

"We are," Amelia said, her heart pounding with fear.

"Please, sit down." The doctor sat in one of the chairs along the adjoining wall. His expression was serious, his brow wrinkled in concern. "Here's where we are at the moment. It's clear that Jessica has a broken back. What we're uncertain of is the extent of any internal injuries she may have suffered. We've stabilised her the best we can at this point. Now we need to send her for an MRI scan before we can decide what else we can do for her."

"She's going to be all right, though, Doctor?" Amelia's father asked.

"I can't lie to you. As much as I'd like to keep your hopes up, I think you should be prepared for the worst. A fall from a horse can be life-threatening in itself. With her injuries and the fact that she's still unconscious—well, that's simply adding to our concerns and frustrations. Bear with us until we see what's going on inside. I want to assure you that she's in the best place possible, and we'll do everything we can to make her comfortable in the hope she regains consciousness soon."

"Thank you, Doctor. Please keep us informed when you can," Amelia said, clasping her mother's hand tighter.

"Is your daughter married?" the doctor asked Amelia's father.

"Yes, her husband has been informed, and we're hoping he'll show his face soon."

"Dad! That's totally unfair," Amelia said. "Sorry, Doctor. Yes, he's aware. I've just rung him, but his phone went through to voicemail. As soon as he receives that message, I'm sure he'll be here soon. He's in Liverpool on business, you see."

"I see," the doctor said. "I'd better get on and organise things. Once Jessica has had the scan, she'll be moved to the Intensive Care Unit. They'll keep an eye on her twenty-four hours a day."

"Thank you for the update, Doctor. Please do your best for her. We don't want to lose her."

"We will. No one in this hospital likes losing a patient." With that, he smiled and left the room.

The family sat around for the next few hours until Wesley finally showed up, looking distraught. He hugged Amelia and her mother then shook her father's reluctant hand. "What's the news? Have you seen her?"

Amelia gave a faint smile. "Thanks for coming back so quickly. She needs us all to be here."

Wesley frowned. "What's that supposed to mean?"

"She's having an MRI scan, then they're going to move her to the Intensive Care Unit. She has a broken back. I know we shouldn't speculate, but when I hear that, I immediately think that she'll be paralysed for the rest of her life."

Wesley ran a hand through his short black hair. "What? That damn horse needs a bullet in its head."

"There's no good speaking like that, Wesley Porter," her mother said. "If it wasn't for that animal going back to alert the staff at the stables, she could've been lying in that forest for hours, if not days."

"Sorry. I didn't mean it, Mary. I'm just lashing out. My God, poor Jessica. I'm going to find the doctor, ask what's going on." He walked towards the door.

"Please don't cause any trouble, Wesley. The doctors and staff have a job to do. The doctor promised he would keep us informed."

Wesley paced in a circle close to the door.

Finally, it opened, and the doctor who had updated them earlier walked into the room. "I'm so sorry for keeping you waiting. Your daughter is now settled in the Intensive Care Unit. I'll show you where that is so you can see her."

Amelia and her mum jumped to their feet.

"What about the scan, Doctor? Did it make anything clearer?" Amelia inclined her head as she asked the question.

"Yes and no. There's no internal bleeding to contend with, and that's a blessing in itself. However, I can't lie to you. Several vertebrae are broken, and there is definite spinal damage visible on the scan. Your daughter remains in critical condition and is still unconscious. That's what is worrying us the most at present. It's possibly her body wanting to shut down in order to repair itself. Please, don't be alarmed when you see her. She's hooked up to several machines to monitor her vitals."

"That sounds bad, Doc. What are her odds?" Wesley asked, his manner forthright and business-like.

"I'm really not one for putting odds on a person's life, sir. Let's just leave it a few days to see what we're truly dealing with before we reassess the situation. She's in the best hands possible. I can assure you of that."

"She better be," Wesley said, glaring at the doctor.

"Stop it, Wesley. Don't make this worse than it already is. The doctor and his staff are doing their very best," her mum said.

Wes's shoulders dropped. "I'm sorry. That was uncalled-for. As you can imagine, I'm worried about my wife's condition. Striking out at you guys won't help matters."

"Apology accepted, and I can totally understand how you must be feeling at this time as the uncertainty mounts. Come on, I'll take you up to see her now."

CHAPTER TWO

When Amelia laid eyes on her sister, she gasped. The others gasped as well as she approached the hospital bed. Jessica's face was pale and bruised, swollen around the eyes. Her head was swathed in bandages, and tubes were coming out of her nose.

"Hello, Sis, how are you doing?" She'd recently read in a magazine how important it was for an unconscious person to hear their loved ones' voices. It helped the recovery, according to the article. She turned to look at the other three members of the family all standing at the end of the bed, afraid to approach it. "Come on, guys, come closer. Let her know that we're all here. Speak to her."

Her mother was the first to step forward. She rounded the bed and lifted her daughter's hand in her own. "Hello, darling, Jess. Come back, sweetheart. We miss you."

Amelia gave her mother a reassuring smile then faced her father. "Your turn, Dad."

Her father shook his head and whispered, "I can't. That's just not Jess. I can't speak to someone who looks nothing like my daughter."

Clearly stunned by his words, Amelia's mother walked towards her husband and stood in front of him. "That's utter nonsense, Gerald. If you're thinking that way, then you're telling us that you've given up on our daughter. If that's the case, you should leave this hospital at once. I won't have it—do you hear me? No one gives up on my child. *No one*. She deserves to have our love and support. That's the only thing that will bring her through this."

"I hear what you're saying, Mary. However, I still can't bring myself to accept that she'll never walk again."

"Then go. I can't be around such a selfish, ignorant person," her mother told him, raising her voice.

Amelia stood between her parents. "Mum, Dad, please don't make a scene here. Mum, we have to accept that's the way Dad feels at the moment. He's confused, and his emotions are all over the place.

Please don't fall out about this. Jess's recovery is going to be hard enough as it is without you two being at each other's throats all the time."

"Listen to your daughter, Gerald. She's talking a lot of sense. We need to pull together, not push each other apart." She faced Jessica and pointed. "That is Jessica in there. Our daughter, the person we have loved and cherished for the past forty-two years. Don't give up on her now, not when she needs us the most." Her mother took her dad's hand and persuaded him to step closer towards his injured daughter. "Talk to her. Tell her how much she means to you."

He shook his head. "I can't, love. I'm sorry, but I just can't do it."

"Don't force him, Mum," Amelia whispered, taking up her place on the other side of the bed again. She turned to glance at Wesley and beckoned him to join her. He looked out of his depth, like her father, and she expected a similar reaction, but he surprised them all by breaking down. He buried his head in his wife's lap and sobbed, saying over and over how sorry he was. Amelia almost choked on the large lump that had developed in her throat. She patted her brother-in-law on the back as he sobbed. It was heartbreaking to see how upset he was. "Let it out, Wes. We all feel the same way. On the other hand, it's important for us to remain positive and strong for Jess's sake. I refuse to give up on her."

"I'm not giving up on her. I feel guilty, like this is my fault some-how. I was the one who bought her that damn horse in the first place. If I had ignored her pleas to own one then she would still be with us today."

Amelia forced him to stand upright and gripped his shoulders. "She *is* still with us. In mind, body, and soul. I'm begging you not to give up on her. She needs our undivided support to enable her to get through this. Why can't you all understand how important it is to remain positive?"

A nurse who was passing by the bed stopped to introduce herself. "Hi, I'm Sandra. Jessica will be in my care. You're right—it's vitally important that you remain positive. Patients always pick up on any negativity, as well as the positivity, around them. I'm sure she'll regain consciousness soon. We'll know more when that happens. We'll take care of her. Please be assured of that. This is a ward full of highly trained, competent staff."

"Pleased to meet you, Sandra. Sorry you experienced my family having a mini-meltdown, but we're just concerned."

"I assure you it happens more frequently than we'd care to admit. It comes as a severe shock to family members to see their loved ones in such a state. Be aware that the unconscious mind knows what is going on around it, though. I'll be at my desk if you have any questions. Don't hesitate to ask. That's what we're here for. Well, that and to care for the patients, of course," she added with a smile then she continued on her journey back to her desk.

"She seems lovely," her mum stated, smiling as she watched the nurse walk away from them.

"She does. Now, come on, Dad, Wes—you heard what the nurse said. We need to remain positive and upbeat all the time, for Jess's sake."

Both men nodded but didn't reply.

As the hours dragged by, Amelia found herself mesmerised by the breathing apparatus helping to keep her sister alive.

At three o'clock, Wes announced, "I'm going home. I need to be there when Cathy returns from school."

"We understand. Send her our love," her mum replied. She approached her son-in-law and pecked him on the cheek. "Will you come back later? We'll be here for the rest of the day and into the night, providing the staff don't kick us out."

"Do you think I should bring Cathy to see her mum? I'm confused. I have no idea how to handle a teenager in such instances. Jess is the cool-headed one between us. She understands Cathy far better than I do."

"Do what's best for the both of you. Sit Cathy down, tell her carefully what has occurred. My advice would be not to tell her the extent on her mother's injuries from the word go. She'll want to come and visit her. I'm sure of that. Try and dissuade her gently. We'll ring you if there's any change."

Wesley kissed her mum on the cheek and hugged her then he walked off the ward.

Amelia shook her head. "He's shell-shocked. Maybe I should have offered to drive him home."

"I'm sure once he gets a bit of fresh air and focusses his mind on what he has to do, he'll be fine. I'm worried about Cathy, though. You know how forthright his manner can be at times. I hope he shows his daughter some compassion when he tells her."

"I think you're underestimating how much he loves Cathy, Mum. I'm sure he'll be fine."

"I'm going to get us all a cup of coffee. Does anyone want a sandwich?" her dad asked.

"A coffee will do fine for me. Thanks, Dad."

"I'll come with you." Her mum took her husband's hand and walked through the swing doors of the unit, leaving Amelia alone with her sister.

Despite the strength she had shown in front of the rest of her family, once she found herself alone, Amelia struggled to suppress her fear. "Please don't die on us, Jess. I know I should be talking positively, but seeing you like this…well, it's hard. Remember when we were kids and you visited me in hospital after I had my tonsils out? You're the one who kept telling me over and over that I would get better soon, and I did. I'm trying to conjure up that same spirit you expressed back then, but it's hard. I want you to get better—of course I do. However, with a broken back, I know your motions will be limited. I fear your zest for life will diminish. I know how depressed that will make you feel. I want you to know that whatever the outcome, I will always remain by your side, to help you through this and any physio you're going to be put through to help you walk again. Just come back to us, sweetie."

A gentle hand touched her shoulder. The nurse spoke quietly, "Sorry, I didn't mean to startle you. You're doing the right thing by speaking to her, but try not to be dismissive of her abilities just yet until further tests have been carried out. The truth is we don't know what's going on and how damaged her body is right now. Yes, the scans can tell us a certain amount, but I've seen the courage some patients have shown to prove our equipment wrong. If Jess has the will to survive, then she'll do just that."

"Thank you." Amelia grasped her sister's hand and willed her to pull through.

Her parents returned to the ward around ten minutes later and placed a cup of coffee in her hand.

"I bought some sandwiches for later in case we get hungry," her father said, putting the packages on the side table next to Jess.

Around five that evening, there was a change of shift for the nurses, and a middle-aged woman with bright-red hair tied back in a ponytail approached them. "Hello there. I'm Patricia. I'll be on duty for the rest of the evening. Don't hesitate to ask any questions you need answering."

"Thank you. Are you going to check Jess's chart to see if there are any changes?" Amelia asked.

"I will do."

The family watched the nurse check Jess's pulse and note down the numbers on the machines before she smiled at them. "Everything appears to be the same, which should be seen as a positive."

Amelia sighed with relief. "That's good to hear." Over the nurse's shoulder, the door to the unit open, and Wesley and Cathy entered the room. Cathy's red eyes made it obvious she had been crying. Amelia's heart went out to her niece.

The nurse said hello to Wesley and Cathy then left them alone. Cathy tentatively stepped towards the bed, her gaze fixed on her mother and the tubes. Her father placed an arm around her shoulder, but she shrugged it off.

"Hello, love. Come a little closer. Talk to your mum," Amelia said, indicating that Cathy should stand next to her. Cathy was in a daze, focusing firmly on her mother.

"She's not going to survive, is she?" Cathy whispered, a single tear dripping onto her cheek.

After witnessing the way the teenager had shrugged her father off, Amelia chose not to touch her niece. Instead, she smiled and shook her head. "She will survive this, sweetie. We need to remain positive at all times. The nurse has checked all her signs, and they haven't altered either way, so we've got to see that as a good thing. Here, have my seat. We've been talking to her, and she'd love to hear your voice."

Cathy's brow furrowed. "But she can't hear us. She's not even aware that we're here, is she?"

"Apparently, she is aware of us being with her, sweetheart. Just try it. See if you can get a reaction from her."

Cathy sat in the seat and leaned forward. "Mum, are you in there? Please, I don't want you to die. We have so many things I need to do with you before you go. Don't leave us, please. I love you. I might not always show how much I love you, but seeing you lying here is breaking my heart in two. Please, please wake up and be as you were before. I'm scared you're going to die. What will I do without you? We need you to come back to us. Dad needs you—you know how hopeless he is around the house. I'll be a starving teenager in no time if you're not around to cook our meals. Basically, Mum, we need you to care for us. I know how selfish that is, but it's the truth.

I always swore that I would never lie to you… Come back to us. We need you fighting fit and to get better quickly."

Amelia wiped away the tears misting her eyes, and she looked up to see her mother gripping her father's hand tightly as tears ran down her flushed cheeks.

"Do you think that was the right thing to say?" Cathy asked her with uncertainty swimming in her eyes.

"If that was you speaking from the heart, love, then yes, it was the right thing to say. Why don't you hold her hand?"

Cathy hesitantly reached out and retracted a number of times before her hand finally covered her mother's. She pulled it away quickly and glanced up at Amelia. "She's really cold. Should she be that cold? Shouldn't she have a few more blankets on her?"

"She's fine. I'm sure the nurses are monitoring her properly. Your touch will warm her up."

Cathy tried again, and this time, her hand stayed on top of her mother's. "Please, Mum, we need you."

No sooner had Cathy said the words than pandemonium started. The alarms on the machines sounded. Cathy leapt out of her chair and ran into her father's arms. He led the scared teenager out of the unit as the nurse jumped into action.

"I'm going to have to ask you to leave. I've contacted the doctor, and he should be here shortly." The nurse ushered them off the ward.

Within seconds, the doctor sprinted past them. Everyone was in shock, unable to speak. Amelia was at a loss for what to say or do. She didn't know whom to comfort first, her mother or her niece. Cathy threw herself against her father's chest and sobbed.

"It's my fault. If I hadn't spoken to her, she wouldn't have reacted to my words. I'm to blame."

"Hush now. Of course you're not to blame. You mustn't think that," Wesley assured his daughter.

Amelia crossed the corridor and ran her hand down her niece's back. "We don't know what's happened yet. Best not to start blaming ourselves. Let's hear what the doctor has to say first."

Cathy nodded and stared as more staff hurriedly entered the unit.

Amelia left her niece and walked back to her parents. "It looks bad, Mum. I wonder what's going on?"

"Let's not speculate yet, love. The doctor will speak to us soon, I'm sure. Until then, we need to stay calm."

The unit door swung open, and several staff members surrounded Jess's bed as it was wheeled past them down the corridor. His face ashen, the doctor said, "I'm sorry, there must be a complication that we haven't picked up on. We're taking her down for emergency surgery."

"Emergency surgery on what?" Wesley asked.

"Her blood pressure has dropped significantly, leading me to believe she has internal bleeding after all. I'm sorry, but I need to get things moving to try and save her life. I'll be in touch when I can." He rushed away from them.

No one spoke for what seemed like an eternity.

"Internal bleeding? That's bad, right?" Cathy finally asked.

"It would be better not to speculate, love. She's in capable hands," Amelia's mum said, gathering her granddaughter in her arms.

It was several hours before anyone came to speak to the family. The doctor smiled as he approached them, but Amelia could tell that his smile was stitched into place—a fake smile he conjured up when he was about to deliver bad news. Amelia's stomach tied itself into knots.

"Right, the surgery went as well as expected. We believe we've stopped the bleed."

"How did you miss it in the first place?" Wesley snapped.

"Not all bleeds are visible from the outset. It could have been a small tear we missed that erupted when Jess was moved. At this stage, we just don't know. The main thing is that she appears to be stable again. We're bringing her back now. You've all been here a long time—why don't you go home. There's nothing you can do for Jess now. My advice would be go home and get some rest. The truth is we have no idea what lies ahead of us."

"What's that supposed to bloody mean?" Wesley demanded.

"I'm sorry, but that's all that I'm willing to say right now. I apologise if it's not what you want to hear, Mr. Porter."

"That's fine, Doctor," Amelia's mum said, stepping between her son-in-law and the doctor. "We'll go along with what you say and come back tomorrow. Will you ring us if there is any change in the meantime?"

"Of course. I do think it's for the best. There's no point burning yourselves out. There is a long road ahead of all of you. I can't emphasise that enough. Jess is in a poor state. We're doing our utmost to keep her stable. We'll continue to monitor her throughout the night, and the nursing staff have been told to contact me if Jess's condition changes. Let's reassess the situation once her body has recovered from surgery and go from there."

"Thank you, Doctor. We'll go home and get some rest. Would it be all right if we came back first thing?" Amelia's mum asked.

"Absolutely. I'll ensure the nursing staff know." He smiled and walked onto the ward again.

The lift door opened at the end of the hallway, and two porters pushed Jess's bed towards them. The men paused before they deposited Jess back on the ward. Each member of the family kissed Jess's cheek and told her that they loved her, then together, they silently made their way towards the lift.

Once inside, Amelia said, "She looked better than I thought she would."

"Not sure how you worked that one out, Amelia. I thought the opposite," Wesley replied.

Silence ensued for the rest of the journey down to the exit. The family all hugged and went their separate ways. Amelia decided to go home with her parents, not sure if she would cope being in her flat alone all night with only her dreary thoughts to keep her company.

~ ~ ~

The following morning, Amelia rang the hospital first thing to get an update on her sister. The nurse on duty told her she'd had a comfortable night and the doctor was due to see her within the hour.

Amelia and her parents decided to return to the hospital around nine-thirty that morning. They were thrilled to see Wesley already sitting alongside Jess's bed when they arrived.

"No Cathy?" Amelia asked, kissing her brother-in-law on the check before she bent to kiss her sister. "Good morning, Jess. How are you doing today?"

"No. I decided it would be better if I dropped her off to school. I've taken the day off work to be here, though."

"We all have. That's great, Wes. She needs to feel us around her."

"Did you manage to get any sleep?" her mum asked Wes.

"Not much. What about you?"

Her mum smiled. "Not much. It's hard to close your eyes knowing that Jess is in a critical condition. I wonder when the doctor will drop by?"

"I'll check with the nurse, Mum." Amelia walked over to the nurses' station and asked the nurse called Sandra, "Is the doctor due soon? We'd like an update on how Jess is doing if that's possible."

"He should be here soon. He usually visits the ward around ten. Jess is coping well at the moment. No lasting side effects from the surgery she had yesterday."

"That's great to know. We're all very worried about her, as you can imagine. None of us have ever been in this situation before, and it's hard to know what to do for the best."

"You're doing fine. Hopefully, Jess will surprise us all and wake up soon. It's sometimes tougher on the family than it is on the patients at this stage. A different matter entirely once the patients regain consciousness, of course. That's when our work really begins."

"I'm sure. Thank you for all you've done for my sister so far. It truly is appreciated."

"We know it is," the nurse replied, laying an appreciative hand on Amelia's arm.

Amelia returned to her family. Something inside her told her that Jess was past the worst and would regain consciousness soon, but she hoped that didn't turn out to be wishful thinking.

A few moments later, the doctor arrived. He greeted everyone with a cautious smile and assessed Jess's chart before he spoke to them. "Good morning, all. Jess is doing fairly well so far. Although, it's still early days yet."

"Any idea when she'll wake up, Doctor?" Wes asked.

"No. The body is very complex, and not everyone reacts the same. Her body will guide her and wake itself up when it can cope better." He left them to continue his rounds.

They spent the rest of the morning reminiscing old times in the hope that hearing their laughter would help Jess regain consciousness.

At around one that afternoon, Jess's machine flatlined. The family was rushed off the ward, and the doctor appeared within a few minutes. The nursing staff worked hard on Jess for the next twenty minutes until the doctor emerged, his shoulders slumped in resignation. "I'm sorry. We did all we could, but her body couldn't deal with her significant injuries."

Wes took a few steps forward. "But you told us this morning she was getting better."

"I'm not sure I said that exactly. I felt she was no worse than yesterday. Sometimes the body shows signs of improvement before it goes into decline. We have no way of knowing which way things are going to go. I'm sorry, Jess just wasn't strong enough to cope with the pain she was suffering."

Amelia comforted her mother as the shock finally gave way to the tears. Although she was devastated by her sister's passing, she felt relieved that she had gone. She realised how debilitating it would have been for Jess to have been possibly confined to a wheelchair for the rest of her life. She wouldn't wish that on anyone, especially someone as active as Jess.

M A Comley

CHAPTER THREE

Kayli Bright crept around the house that morning, not wishing to wake Mark. They were still working opposite shifts. He often got home from his shift at the nightclub as a doorman at gone five in the morning. It was harder than either of them had anticipated when Mark had taken the position. Sundays were different, of course, which they spent mainly in bed. But both of them wanted more than that.

Between them they were trying their hardest to find Mark a more suitable job with better hours, although, he'd said that he loved the job itself. It wasn't what he'd expected, but it was the hours that were getting both of them down. After two months of barely seeing each other for an hour a day, the newlyweds were desperate to spend some quality time together.

Kayli feared what would happen if something didn't come their way soon. It wasn't his fault—he was trying his hardest to find another job, but they were proving too elusive to find.

They'd been through enough turmoil in their lives in the last few years. She loved Mark more than she'd ever loved any other man in her life, but the strain was starting to affect their relationship. Snippy remarks when they saw each other were becoming the norm and getting Kayli down. The more she raised the subject, the more Mark rebelled.

She sat at the kitchen table, mulling over the situation while she ate her toast and drank her first cup of coffee for the day. She was at a loss to know what to do best for both their benefits. She would never dream of giving up her job on the force.

She washed up her plate and cup and set off for work. When she arrived at the station, she was thrilled to see her partner, Dave, doing an Irish jig after he left his car and walked towards her.

"Yes, I'm free. Free and whole again."

Kayli laughed. "I'm glad to see it. How does it feel not having that cast around your leg, matey?"

"It feels wonderful. I had the best night's sleep in ages last night—well, that was after Suranne and I made up for lost time…you know, in the sex department."

Kayli raised her hand. "Whoa! Hang on, Dave. That's too much information for my delicate ears, especially at this hour of the morning."

Dave's cheeks coloured up. "Sorry, boss. It's natural for guys to speak about such things openly."

"Maybe with other guys, but not with me. Got that?"

"Who's rattled your cage? Oh, wait—I know what your sharp tongue is about. You're not getting it, so you're taking it out on me, yes?"

"Wrong! End of conversation. My sex life is my own affair. Right?" Kayli turned on her heel and stomped towards the entrance of the station.

Dave mumbled something indecipherable behind her before his footsteps slowly followed her up the stairs.

She turned mid-flight. "Sorry, Dave, you didn't deserve that. I'm glad you're free again. This should be a joyful occasion, and I've put a dampener on it. Forgive me?"

He swerved to avoid her and grumbled, "Nothing to forgive." Then he chuckled and said, "Race you to the top."

Kayli took the stairs two at a time, but he still made it to the top ahead of her. "You cheated."

"Nope, you're out of shape. Which goes back to our conversation in the car park about sex."

She jabbed him in the stomach, hard enough to make him bend over and cry out in pain. "I warned you to leave it."

He held up his hands and pulled himself upright. "All right, you didn't have to do that so hard."

"Take the hint and leave well alone in future. Let's see what's on the agenda for today. We've had a few crappy cases to deal with lately. I need something with a bit of meat on it to sink my teeth into to get my juices flowing again."

"You're such a carnivore." Dave laughed as they entered the incident room, where Donna and Graeme were already at their desks.

"Hi, guys. Anything juicy for us today?"

Donna shook her head. "Sorry, boss. Nothing as yet. Good to see you off your crutches, Dave. That must be a relief."

"It is. Thanks, Donna."

Kayli raised her hand to prevent him saying anything else. "Donna, did you have to mention it? You're lucky you didn't get the response I did downstairs. I know more about his sex life than I do my own."

The group roared with laughter as Dave's cheeks flared up for a second time that morning. "Ha bloody ha! My lips are sealed on that particular topic from this day forward."

"Can I get that in writing? That way, I can dangle the sheet of paper under your nose as a reminder now and again, just to keep you on track."

"You're full of it today, boss. I feel sorry for Mark if this is the kind of mood you're in around him."

"It's not. You insensitive b…" Anger bubbled to the surface. She avoided saying anything further to Dave and walked over to the vending machine. After choosing a white coffee with one sugar, she left the group and headed for her office.

Donna tutted and said something to Dave. He sounded dumbfounded when he responded to his colleague's telling off. "What did I say? I was only joking. Not my fault she's had a sense-of-humour transplant lately."

Kayli slammed her door shut. It didn't take long for her to regret snapping at her partner. He was right, though—she was wrong to bring her foul mood to work with her. It was totally out of character.

She spent the morning immersed in paperwork and ventured out of her office at around twelve. Then the team went over the case files that were completed and awaiting the next step in the process. The top one caught Kayli's eye. It related to the woman who had attempted to kill Dave by running him down, hence why he'd been on crutches for the past six weeks and driving her nuts. "How do you feel about this, Dave?"

He shrugged. "What can I say? She deserves everything coming her way and more for what she put those poor people through—and for what she did to me, of course."

"Are you going to be able to face her in court?"

He nodded and folded his arms. "Too right. 'Bring it on,' I say. She's going down for life, that one. My evidence will simply be the longest nail in her coffin."

"As long as you're all right about it, that's fine by me. What else have we got, Donna?"

"More court dates that are pending and a few snippets we have to chase up from forensics pertaining to cases that are due to go to court next week. I can do that for you this afternoon, boss. I've got nothing else planned."

"Excellent news. No new cases to deal with at present? I can't believe the people of Bristol are behaving themselves for a change."

Dave tutted. "Famous last words. That's bound to open the bloody floodgates now."

As if on cue, the phone on Donna's desk rang. "Hello. Donna Travis. How may I help?" Donna sat back in her chair and smiled. "Hi, Paula. Long time, no hear. How is married life treating you? Oh right. What can I do for you, in that case? Before you say anything else, I'm going to put your call on speaker, so my boss can hear what you have to say."

Kayli frowned and walked closer to Donna's desk. "Hello, Paula. This is DI Kayli Bright. How can I help you?"

"Hi. Look, first of all, I'm not sure I'm doing the right thing ringing you at all about this, but I couldn't live with myself if I didn't tell someone about what I've discovered."

"We'll decide if we can help once you tell us. Please, don't be nervous," Kayli reassured her.

"I work at Hawthorn Stables. Not sure if you know where that is?"

Donna quickly typed the name into the computer and nodded. "I've got it up on the screen, Paula. Carry on."

"Well, a few days ago, one of our customers came to pick up her horse, took him out for a ride, and had a dreadful accident. She fell off her horse. The sad part is that yesterday, she died in hospital. I've been tasked with cleaning up the stable where she kept her horse, and well… I've found something that doesn't sit right with me. I was hoping Donna would help me out, perhaps tell me I'm being foolish or whatever before I go and see my boss about it."

"We'll try and help if we can, Paula," Donna said. "What have you found?"

Paula sighed several times before she spoke again. "I think Jessica—that's the lady who died—well…they recovered her saddle and when I looked it over…umm…I think her saddle was tampered with."

Kayli's eyebrow shot up. "Are you sure about that? Could the saddle have been damaged during the fall?"

"I'm pretty sure. Oh God, I'm going to get into trouble for contacting you about this… Maybe I've done the wrong thing."

"No, you're right to ring us, Paula. Do you want me to come down and take a gander? I'm willing to do that if only to put your mind at rest."

"It's up to you. All I can say is that in my experience, I've never seen a saddle damaged in this way before. I'm also aware that Jessica was a very experienced rider, and it would have taken a lot to have knocked her off her horse. She fell on a fallen tree trunk and ended up breaking her back. It was Nutmeg, her horse, who returned to the stables by itself that prompted us to send out a search party for her. I can't believe she's dead. That type of thing just doesn't happen around here, you have to take my word on that."

"Okay, I'm listening, and I don't like what I'm hearing. My partner and I will head off now and be with you in around thirty minutes."

"Oh my, the boss will be furious that I've gone behind her back. Is there any way you can keep me out of it? You know, say you're following up on Jessica's accident or something along those lines?"

"Leave it to us. We'll be subtle, I promise you. Just act surprised when you see us."

"Thank you. I hate being underhanded like this. I hope I'm not giving you the wrong impression."

"Not at all. I respect your honesty and admire you trying to do what's right. We'll see you soon, Paula."

"Okay. Bye for now."

Donna ended the call. "That's so unlike Paula. I hope she's wrong. I dread to think the hassle this could cause, not only for Paula but for the poor victim's family, as well."

"You're right. It's a tough situation to tackle. We'll tiptoe around the issue to begin with. Don't worry. Your friend did the right thing getting in touch with us. Dave, are you ready? We should leave now."

"Ready and raring to go. Fit enough to chase anyone who decides to leg it out of guilt, too." He grinned broadly and did another jig.

Kayli shook her head in despair. "Hopefully it won't come to that, but we won't know that until we get there. While we're gone,

Donna, can you do some background checks on the stables and the owner for me?"

"I was thinking along the same lines, boss. I'll have the information ready for you when you get back."

~ ~ ~

Kayli and Dave arrived at the large stables on the edge of the village at Failand. "Looks like a well-established place. I envisioned it being smaller for some reason," Kayli said.

"Not heard of this place myself. Not that I do a lot of horse riding in my spare time, but Suranne used to at one point, before she had the baby."

"I'd advise her not to take it up again in the near future, at least until we figure out what's going on around here. We might dig up some horrifying tales in our quest to find the truth."

"Crap, I hope not, for the owner's sake."

"Let's take this nice and easy, all right?"

"Hey, the ball's in your court, boss. I'm easy with following your lead on this one."

They left the car and walked into the stable's courtyard, where several people had their horses tied up outside the stables and were either hosing their animals down or grooming them. They approached the lady nearest to them and Kayli asked, "Sorry to interrupt. Can you tell me where I'd find the owner?"

"The office is just around the corner. You can't miss it," the young woman said, pointing over to the left, past the last stable in view.

"Much appreciated, thank you."

They walked past the rest of the stalls and located the office straight away. Kayli opened the half-glazed door and stepped into a reception area that was no bigger than twenty-feet square. A younger blonde lady sat at the nearest desk, and an older woman was sorting through paperwork at the rear desk. Both women looked up as Kayli and Dave entered.

"Hello there. Would either of you be the owner of this establishment?" Kayli enquired.

The older woman stood and approached them, a smile stretching her ruby lips apart. "That would be me for my sins. I'm Susan Lord. How may I help you?"

Kayli flashed her warrant card in the woman's face. "DI Kayli Bright, and this is my partner, Dave Chaplin. It's just a general enquiry really. We heard about an incident that happened here a few days ago, and we're following up on that."

"You're talking about the accident Jessica Porter had whilst out riding her horse?"

"That's the one. Are you aware that Jessica has since lost her life?"

Susan's head dropped slightly as sadness touched her features. "Yes, painfully aware. Jessica was not only a customer of mine, but a dear friend, too. Shocking news for all of us to comprehend."

"As with enquiries of this nature, we've been tasked with just ensuring everything was as it should have been regarding the equipment Jessica was using. Would it be acceptable to take a look at her saddle? I'll gladly obtain a warrant if you object, of course."

"Nonsense. Why would I object? I'll take you over to the stable she used for Nutmeg during his stay with us."

"Is the horse still here?"

"Sadly not. Wesley, her husband, dropped by yesterday to inform me that someone would be picking Nutmeg up, as he'd sold him. To tell you the truth, I was shocked when he told me that. It all happened so quickly."

"Within a day of his wife's death—that does seem odd." Kayli nodded at Dave, motioning for him to jot down the information.

"On the one hand, I can totally understand where he's coming from. It would be a dreadful reminder coming here every day to take care of the horse and being reminded that if Jessica hadn't fallen, she would still be with us today. On the other hand, I know Cathy loved Nutmeg as much as Jess did. Not sure how Cathy has taken what her father has done, if she knows, that is."

"It's a difficult dilemma for sure."

"I'll take you to the stable now. I asked one of the staff to clear it out this morning. I need to get the stable filled pretty swiftly. Empty spaces are lost money to a livery owner, as you can imagine."

"I can. So Jessica's equipment is still here then? Isn't that strange? I mean, I would have thought it would have been sold along with the horse, or am I misreading things here?"

"No. That rarely happens. Riders usually stick with the equipment they already have. They get used to riding in the same saddle—I suppose it's akin to wearing in a pair of shoes. He'll probably end up selling it on eBay or something. I can't see Cathy wanting it," Susan added with a shrug. "I'll show you where everything is, and you can judge for yourself."

Kayli and Dave followed Susan across the yard to a stable that smelled of fresh hay. She led them to a small room at the rear and pointed out the equipment arranged neatly on a small table. "It's all there. Looks like Paula has finished cleaning up in here."

"Would it be possible to speak to Paula before we go?"

"Of course. Any reason why?"

"Just a few enquiries about the equipment and if it's all here—that type of thing."

"I'll track her down and send her in to see you. Mind if I get back to work?"

"That's fine. We don't want to hold you up."

"No problem. Always happy to help the police with their enquiries. You know where I am if you need me."

"Thanks, you're very kind."

As soon as Susan left the stable, Kayli turned to Dave and whispered, "That's weird, the husband selling the horse so quickly."

"I was thinking the same. Wouldn't he have other things to worry about if his wife had just died? Seems a little callous to me."

"My thoughts exactly. I hope the daughter is the forgiving type. I'd be pretty irate if a member of my family did something like that so soon after one of my relatives had died."

"Maybe he's the organised type. Wanted everything done and dusted before he had to sort out the funeral details." Dave flung his arms out to his sides. "Who knows what goes on in someone's head at a time like this?"

"Something we need to delve into nevertheless."

"Hello, is anyone in here?" a female called out.

Kayli emerged from the back room and entered the stable to find a young blonde woman wearing leggings and a padded gilet over a tartan shirt. "Hi, are you Paula?"

"I am. The boss said you wanted to see me," she said, obviously keeping up the pretence in case they were overheard.

"That's right. If you'd like to come through to the other room, I'd appreciate it."

Once the three of them were in the smaller room, Kayli closed the door behind them and shook Paula's hand. "Hi, Paula. Thanks for ringing us. Can you show us what you found?"

"Hi, thanks for coming. I might be wrong about this but I'd rather appear foolish than let something like this slip by without getting mentioned. Here, this is called the billet strap. It's how a rider attaches the saddle to the horse. To me, it looks like the strap was cut with something." She pointed at a leather strap approximately an inch in width.

"Hmm…couldn't it have just worn through age?"

"I don't think so. The saddle is relatively new. I remember Jessica telling me that once her grandmother's inheritance came through, that was going to be the first thing on her shopping list—a new super-duper, all-whistles saddle."

Dave bent down to inspect the leather strap and nodded. "Seems like a cut to me. Admittedly, it's frayed a little at the end, but maybe someone cut it three quarters of the way through in the hope that would do the trick."

Kayli placed her thumb and forefinger around her chin as she thought. "I'm not so sure. How likely would it be for a leather strap to break after a few months of use, Paula?"

"I've yet to come across anything like this happening. Maybe there could have been a fault in the leather, but it's highly unlikely. Not something I've come across ever before—and I've been working with horses in one way or another for the past twenty years as a rider and a stable hand."

"Okay, that's certainly sparked my interest. Were you here when Nutmeg was sold?"

"Yes. Jess's husband turned up with another man, along with a horsebox. None of us knew what was going on until they loaded Nutmeg into the box. We all watched as the horsebox left the yard. It was then that Wesley announced that he'd sold Nutmeg to a friend of his."

"As quickly as that? Did he say why?"

"He said that he was struggling, knowing that the horse was still around when his wife wasn't."

"So he blamed his wife's death on an innocent animal?"

"That's how it seemed to me. He totally forgot that if it hadn't been for Nutmeg returning to the yard, we wouldn't have learnt about the accident in the first place. I was shocked at the speed it all happened, to be honest with you."

Kayli nodded. "It does seem a little too frantic to me. I wonder if his daughter is aware of Nutmeg's departure?"

"I don't think so. Cathy is going to be mortified when she finds out. Amelia will be, too."

"Amelia? Who's she?"

"Jessica's sister. She's only just started coming down here."

"I don't suppose you have any contact details for her—either phone or possibly her address?"

"I haven't. Susan might have it in the office."

Kayli nodded. "Okay, I'll ask when I go back in there. Just a moment. I need to make a quick call." She opened the door to the stable again and walked to the far side. Close to the door, she withdrew her phone from her pocket. She dialled a number she knew by heart and waited.

"Caroline Stacy."

"Hey, Caroline. It's Kayli. Do you have time for a brief chat? I have a dilemma on my hands."

"I've always got time for you. What's up?"

"I'm at a stable where an accident occurred…okay, that's wrong. The horse involved in the incident was stabled here when it threw its rider, its owner. Unfortunately, the owner, Jessica Porter, has since died from her injuries in the last few days."

"Can I stop you there? I have her down on my list for a PM today. Are you telling me you think this wasn't an accident?"

Kayli sighed heavily. "It looks that way. One of the stable hands here was getting the stable ready for a new arrival when she spotted something suspicious on the saddle. I've come down to check it out, and it would appear the billet strap has been tampered with. When the horse either jumped the tree trunk in the woods or possibly reared up, that's when Jessica fell off the horse. She landed on the trunk, hence breaking her back. My take is that this was a deliberate act."

"Ouch, okay. Do you need me to come down there?"

"Not really. I think it would be a waste of time to be honest—the stable has been thoroughly cleaned. However, I was wondering if one of your team could come down and assess the saddle for me. Possibly take it in as evidence?"

"Of course. I think you're right if you have suspicions surrounding the woman's death. I can get someone down there now if you like."

"You're amazing. That would be a big help. I haven't officially taken over the investigation as I don't think our guys were involved, so if you can send me the PM report, I'd appreciate it."

"By what you've said you have a right to investigate the case. I'll do all I can to help, you know that. Have you visited the scene of the accident yet?"

"Not yet. Dave and I will head out that way once we've finished here. I'll wait around for your technician to show up before we leave." She lowered her voice to say the next part. "Here's the thing. The woman only died yesterday, but almost immediately after her death, the husband got rid of the horse. Don't you think that's strange?"

"Yes and no. The wonders of dealing with grief. No one knows how anyone is going to react to a situation. A word of warning going forward for you—I wouldn't take the husband's reaction as a malicious act."

"Thanks, I'll take that on board during the investigation. I'm going to get on now, interview a few people around here before I locate the crime scene, and see that for myself."

"I'll send my guy over for a nose-around and get back to you soon. Good luck."

"Thanks. We'll probably need it." Kayli ended the call and returned to the small room at the back where Dave and Paula were waiting. "I've just rung the local pathologist to get her opinion on things. She's sending a technician down to go over the saddle."

Dave nodded. "Okay, that seems logical. It's a shame this place is now looking spick-and-span for a new resident. Whoever is responsible for tampering with the saddle might have left some valuable DNA or clues for us to chance."

Kayli shrugged. "We have to work with what we have, Dave."

"I'm sorry. That's my fault. The boss ordered me to clean it up as soon as possible so it's ready for the new arrival, whenever that may be."

"Sorry, I didn't mean anything disparaging by my statement," Dave apologised, sheepishly.

Kayli dug him in the ribs and smiled at Paula. "You'll have to forgive my partner—he's fond of putting his size tens in his mouth."

"I'm a size nine, actually, and I don't do it that often," Dave said.

"Thankfully, otherwise you wouldn't be my partner. I can guarantee you that. I'm sorry. I've just had a thought. I need to ring the DCI, run this past her first before we take on the case. I'm sure she'll be fine but I'd like to do it all the same now that I've put the wheels in motion with the path lab."

Dave nodded. "Good idea. Want me to start asking around?"

"Not yet, Dave. I've got a feeling we're going to have to tread carefully on this one initially." Kayli placed the call to the station and gave DCI Sandra Davis the lowdown of what they had encountered before asking for permission to carry on with the investigation.

"Hands down, lady. If you think there's evidence that the saddle was tampered with and the victim died because of the injuries that occurred during the fall, then yes, you definitely, one hundred percent have my permission to turn this case from a general enquiry into a murder case. How terrible. I wonder who would do such a thing."

"That's what I intend to find out, boss."

"You said the husband has sold the horse?"

"Yes. I thought it was strange, perhaps the strangest part of all this. That was until the pathologist pointed out that grief can be the cause of people making unusual decisions at a time of a loved one's passing."

"Maybe. Okay, so you're going full steam ahead with this one. You know where I am if you need a chat."

"Thanks, boss. Dave and I will investigate things thoroughly here before we make our way over to interview the relatives."

"I don't have to tell you to go easy, do I?"

"I will, boss. Speak later."

Dave appeared by her side when she placed her phone in her pocket. "Want me to get on to Donna to start digging into the family's background?"

"Good idea. DCI Davis has given us her blessing to forge ahead with the investigation. We'll tread carefully where the family are concerned."

"So what's next?"

"We need to hang around here for a while until the SOCO guy arrives. In the meantime, I want to have another chat with the owner of the stables, see if she has any idea of how Jessica's saddle was tampered with. Then I think we should go and take a look at the scene where the accident happened. Paula, do you know where that is?"

"Roughly, I can show you where I think it took place."

"Excellent. Why don't you carry on with what you're supposed to be doing, and I'll track you down when we're ready to head over that way?"

"I'll be around the courtyard, mucking out the stables, so I won't be far."

Kayli and Dave watched Paula leave the stable, her shoulders slumped.

"What's your gut instinct telling you on this case?" Dave enquired.

They left the stable and walked towards the office.

"Too soon to tell yet, partner. You obviously have a view on this. Otherwise, you wouldn't have raised the point."

"Nothing concrete. I'm veering towards the husband just because of his actions so far."

"It's too soon to make a judgement call like that, Dave, although I appreciate where you're coming from. Let's play it cool on that front for now. I think we're going to have to be cautious every step of the way on this case. Let's keep our minds open and our eyes alert at all times. A knowing glint in someone's eye or a disguised smile could be the undoing of the culprit."

"I'm prepared to follow your lead on this one, boss." Dave grinned broadly.

She shook her head and smiled. "In other words, this case will be broken or fail, and the onus will lay firmly on my shoulders. Right?"

Dave winked at her and they entered the office.

Susan Lord looked their way when she saw them. "Did you find what you were searching for, Inspector?"

"We did. And more. I have to inform you that we'll be treating Jessica Porter's death as suspicious."

Susan left her chair and rushed towards them. "What on earth is that supposed to mean?"

"Our initial findings have uncovered that all is not well with Jess's saddle. We'll be conducting our enquiries once the scenes of crimes officers have confirmed our findings. In other words, we suspect that Jessica was murdered."

Susan swept a hand over her colourless face. "No. I don't believe it. Who would do such a terrible thing? To Jess, of all people?"

"Are you telling me that you find that hard to believe?"

"Of course I am. Jess was one of the sweetest people I know. Very family orientated. She loved her daughter and worshipped the ground Wesley stood on. Why would anyone deliberately set out to hurt her? Kill her, even? I find it very hard to fathom. Sorry."

"You knew her well then?"

"Yes, we've been friends for years. In fact, we used to go to school together. We were in the same class back then. We lost contact with each other until Jess walked in here a few years ago, enquiring about stabling Nutmeg. We hit it off straight away again, and I was proud to consider her one of my best friends."

"Did she confide in you?"

"Sometimes. What are you getting at?" Susan asked, tilting her head as if confused.

"Did she mention recently if she was troubled by anything in particular?"

Susan paused to think the question over for a few moments before she replied, "No, nothing is coming to mind. I would even go as far to say that she seemed far happier recently than she has done in years."

"That's odd. So you're telling me that she's had problems to deal with in the past. Is that right?"

"I wouldn't say 'problems' exactly. Her grandmother had Alzheimer's for a few years before she died. As Jess wasn't working, she volunteered to take on the brunt of responsibility for her grandmother's care. I saw her change in that time. It was as if she had taken on too much and was scared to tell the family she'd made a mistake. Anyway, after her grandmother died, she was upset, of course—who wouldn't be? However, I also saw a heavy weight lift from her shoulders."

"That must have been hard for her to contend with. Did the rest of her family back her or leave the caring solely to Jessica?"

"Sorry if I misled you. They all pitched in, but Jessica was a martyr and refused to let the rest of the family care for her gran as much as she did. Her grandmother had always been special to Jessica. When her grandfather died of a heart attack a few years ago, her grandmother struggled to get used to living alone. That was until Jess stepped in. Unfortunately, her grandmother's health soon started to deteriorate. Jess was the type of person who refused to give up, and she was determined to ensure her grandmother's time left on earth was pleasurable. She used to come here to relieve her stress.

Riding Nutmeg was her guilty pleasure when the family took over caring for her grandmother for a few hours to give her a reprieve."

"And how did her husband react to Jess being preoccupied with looking after her grandmother all the time?"

"Wesley was great. He took over doing the house chores and caring for Cathy, their teenage daughter. She's a bright girl. I predict she has a great future ahead of her... At least she had before this happened. Who knows what devastating effect her mother's death will have on her future?"

"It's very sad. We've yet to visit the family. Would it be possible for you to give me their address?"

"Of course. I'll sort that out for you now." Susan rushed back to her corner of the room and opened the filing cabinet close to her desk. She extracted a manila folder and jotted down an address on a sheet of paper before depositing the file back in the filing cabinet.

As Susan walked towards her, Kayli asked, "Do you think it was strange that Jessica's husband got rid of the horse the way he did?"

Susan's chest inflated as she sucked in a breath. "It's really not my place to voice an opinion on the matter. I'm sorry."

"I appreciate what you're saying. I'm simply trying to work out the logic behind such an act. Wouldn't Cathy object to him selling her mother's horse like that? Does Cathy ride?"

"I can't really say either way, Inspector. Cathy rarely comes down here, and she didn't seem the type of teenager who was interested in riding."

"What about Jess's sister? Amelia, is it? Paula mentioned in passing that she had visited the stables recently. Was that to take up riding?"

"I think she was thinking about it, but although she had the funds, she was struggling to find a horse that she liked."

"If that was the case, and if Wesley was aware of that, then why wouldn't he have given the horse to Amelia?"

Susan shook her head. "That's really something you're going to have to ask him about. If I were in his shoes, then I would have gone down that route rather than farm the horse out to someone I didn't know."

"Do you know who has the horse now?"

"No. I wasn't here when the horsebox arrived. Otherwise, I would have tried to obtain that information to add to my records. But we're just a livery stable where people stable their horses. There's nothing binding in any contracts we have that the owners can't sell their horses. Most people volunteer the information without the need for us asking. Wesley did not do that for reasons known only to himself."

"Well, we'll be sure to ask the question ourselves when we interview him. What about around here? Did everyone get on with Jess?"

Susan seemed shocked by the question. "Yes, of course. I'd be flabbergasted to find out that anyone had a problem with Jess. She was extremely well liked by everyone who worked here. Some of our horse owners treat the staff…indifferently, shall we say? Not Jess. She treated everyone the same, the way she always expected to be treated herself."

"That's reassuring to know. Although I need you to be aware that as the investigation progresses and things come to light, we might have to come back and interview the staff. Would you have any objection to that?"

"Not at all. Our gate is always open for you, if I can put it that way. Do you need to know anything else while you're here?"

"I don't think so at the moment. I need to interview the family before we take matters further. Would it be all right if we borrowed Paula for half an hour? She's promised to show us where the accident occurred. It would be good to see the crime scene for ourselves."

"Of course. She can go with you for as long as necessary. I want to know what happened as much as you guys do."

"Thanks. Can I ask you not to make contact with the family after we leave this office?"

"My lips are sealed. You don't think one of them is responsible for her death, do you?"

Kayli shrugged. "We really can't discount anyone at this early stage. It's imperative that we keep an open mind. Thanks for being so honest with me. We promise not to keep Paula too long."

Kayli and Dave left the office. Paula was carrying a large sack of food across the courtyard.

"We're ready when you are, Paula," Kayli called out.

"I'll be with you in two minutes. Just got to feed a couple of horses."

Waiting for the stable hand to join them, Kayli and Dave debated what to do next.

"Jot down the order of things we need to do first, Dave."

He withdrew his notebook, flipped it open at a blank page, and poised his pen at the ready. "Go on then. I take it going to the scene should be at the top of the to-do list?"

"Bravo. Then I think we should shoot over and see Wesley at the family home, if he's there."

"Where else would he be?" Dave asked, looking up from his notes. "Surely he wouldn't be at work? Not so soon after his wife's death."

"I don't know. I left my crystal ball at home on the dressing table this morning."

"You managed to bring your sharp tongue and sarcasm with you, though," he replied, disgruntled.

"Sorry, that was harsh. We won't know until we get there, matey. Next, I think we should go and see Amelia and possibly Jess's parents, to get their take on the marriage et cetera."

"A day and a half of interviewing the family members in that case."

"It's gonna take however long it takes, Dave. What's your problem today?"

"Me? No problem with me, except now that I'm fully fit, I'm dying to test out if I'm able to outrun a criminal."

Kayli tutted. "You can, mentally. That's the type of case this is going to turn out to be. I can feel it in my bones."

CHAPTER FOUR

Paula smiled as she crossed the yard towards them, pulling her body warmer around her to ward off the wind that had struck up. "I'm ready. Sorry for the delay. The horses would have created merry hell if I hadn't fed them at their usual time."

"Not a problem. Do you want to go by car, or shall we set off on foot?"

"It's not too far. The entrance to the forest is about a ten-minute walk down the lane, if you're up to it."

"That's fine. We'll walk then. It'll give my partner a chance to exercise his leg."

Paula frowned. "Sorry, I don't understand."

"I've been in a cast for the last six weeks with a broken leg. You'll get used to my boss's sarcasm. Although it does wear a little thin after a while."

Kayli chuckled. "Ignore Misery Guts. We make a good team. I promise. Do you mind running through what happened on the day of the accident again for us?"

By the time she had gone over what she knew of the events leading up to Jessica Porter's accident, Paula's eyes were watery with unshed tears. "Please do your best to find out who did this to Jess. She was such a sweet lady. It's terrifying to think someone would kill a lady as nice as Jess. Worse still if that person turns out to be someone who knew her."

"I assure you that we'll do our very best to ensure whoever is responsible is punished. Hopefully, it won't take us long to find the culprit."

Kayli had always regarded forests as eerie places, and the one where Jessica Porter had suffered her accident was no exception. If anything, it was more unsettling than any of the others she had visited.

They hadn't gone very far when Paula pointed at a large trunk blocking the forest path. "That's it. That's where Jess fell. My take is that she managed to persuade Nutmeg to jump the trunk, and that's when she slipped off. Either that, or something spooked him when he landed on the other side, and her reared up. Poor Jess wouldn't have stood a chance of avoiding the trunk when she fell. Every rider falls at least a few times throughout their riding career—we're taught how to fall and, more importantly, how to avoid sustaining a bad injury. But she wouldn't have stood a chance of adhering to any advice she'd been given when she saw that trunk looming beneath her." Paula shuddered.

Kayli reached out and rubbed the top of Paula's arm. "Try not to think about it too much."

Looking sad, Paula said, "Easier said than done. I can't help feeling responsible in some way. I'm the one who always took care after Nutmeg—you know, mucks out his stable. At least I used to. It's so sad that he's no longer around. I miss him. He was such a sweet horse."

"I know. I'm so sorry. Please don't feel responsible. Are you saying that you were the one who put Jess's saddle away after every ride?"

"Yes, always. I needn't have done it, as that task is usually up to the owners, but I volunteered to do it for Jess because she always seemed in a rush to get home. Between you and me, she's the only owner who thought to give me a card at Christmas with a gift in it—only twenty pounds, but I really appreciated her generosity. So I went out of my way to treat her and Nutmeg well."

"She is coming across as a nice lady. Let's see what we can do to find the person responsible for taking her life in that case. Can you think back? Maybe someone new had entered Nutmeg's stable recently?"

"I've thought about that but I honestly can't think of a time anyone else was near his stable."

"What happens when the stables are closed?"

"The gates are shut, and there's CCTV cameras in place. Didn't Susan mention that when you saw her earlier?"

"No, and I forgot to ask. I'll rectify that when I get back. Can we have a quick hunt around—maybe in the undergrowth—to see if we can find anything that may have spooked the horse?"

"I came out here after I heard what had happened and did just that but failed to find anything. I'm willing to take a second hunt around if it would help."

Kayli smiled and nodded. "Just a brief one."

The three of them dug around the undergrowth close to the trunk on both sides but found nothing.

"Wouldn't SOCO want to come and see the scene for themselves, boss?" Dave asked.

"I pondered that but dismissed it. I think they'll be more interested in the saddle rather than where the accident took place. It's obvious, to me at least, that was the main contributing factor in Jess's death. I'll have a word with the technician when we return."

"I don't think there's anything here which could have spooked the horse," Dave said, kicking several mounds of leaves on the ground at his feet.

"I agree. Let's head back to the stables."

They walked back in silence, each caught up in their own private thoughts.

Paula went on with her work, and Dave sought out the technician examining the saddle, while Kayli went in search of Susan.

She walked into the office to find Susan at her desk, going through paperwork. "Sorry to interrupt again. During our trip, I asked Paula if it was possible that someone might have got into the stables after hours, and she informed me that the gates are locked and that you have CCTV cameras in place. I spotted one angled at the gates on my way back. Silly question, but do they work, or are they just for show?"

"No, they work."

"Any chance we can take a look at the discs or tapes? We need to know who visited Nutmeg's stable either the day before or on the day Jessica had her accident."

Susan crossed the room to a machine in the corner. "I'm sorry I didn't think about mentioning the CCTV before. My mind is all over the place, as you can imagine."

She flicked through a few disc cases and extracted two, then she handed the cases to Kayli.

"That's brilliant. I'll take a copy and get the originals returned to you ASAP. Let's hope we pick up something useful from these. Can I ask if you noticed if the gates had been tampered with lately?"

"No. I can't say I've noticed that in the slightest. Are you suggesting that someone got in here and did this?"

Kayli looked her in the eye and nodded. "Either that, or someone who worked here did the damage to Jess's saddle."

Susan gasped and covered her mouth. She dropped her hand and shook her head vehemently. "Seriously? No, I don't believe that for a second, Inspector. All my staff are trustworthy."

"Then it must be the former option. I wasn't accusing anyone, merely pointing out the alternatives. Paula seems a really nice girl. Has she worked for you long?"

"Around five years, I suppose. She and Jess got on really well, and this has had a grave impact on her. I've caught her crying a few times while she's been mucking out. Very sad situation."

"She does seem a sensitive soul. Very upset that Nutmeg has left the stables, too."

"We're all sad to see him go, but there really wasn't anything we could have done about that. Had Wesley mentioned his intention to sell the horse, I would have bought Nutmeg myself in a heartbeat. He was such a gentle creature. I truly hope he's gone to a caring home."

"I'll be sure to ask Wesley that when I interview him later. Thanks for the discs. Let's hope we find something on them. How many cameras do you have on site?"

"Only the three. One on the front gates, another on the yard, and another out the back on the manège area. Why out there, I don't know. I was advised to do it that way by the guy who installed the equipment. I kind of got bamboozled into going along with his suggestion."

"Thanks. I'll be in touch soon if I need anything else. These should keep us busy for a while," Kayli said, holding up the disc cases. "I'll check how the SOCO technician is doing then shoot off."

When Kayli entered the stable, she found Dave talking to the technician, who appeared to be packing up his bag, getting ready to leave. "All done here?" she asked.

"Yep, I'm going to take the saddle away with me. Carry out the tests back at the lab. Was there anything else you wanted me to look at while I'm here?"

"I don't think so. Dave's probably told you already that we visited the scene and hunted around there for clues."

"He has. I can take a wander over there if you want me to but I doubt I'll find anything. The saddle seems to be the main piece of evidence and the reason the accident occurred in the first place."

"That was my thinking. When can we expect your results?"

"In a few days. Although, I can give you a brief summary now if you like?"

"Go on, surprise me."

"It would appear that the strap was cut with either a sharp knife or a blade of sorts. Perhaps three quarters of the way through, putting enough stress on it that if anything out of the ordinary happened, it would give way immediately."

"You've confirmed what we had ascertained already. I look forward to reading your in-depth report in a few days. Thanks for coming out here so promptly. As you can imagine, it's extremely important for us to find the culprit as soon as we possibly can."

"Obviously. I'll do my best to get the results back to you quickly."

"Dave will help you out to your car with your equipment." She smiled at her partner. "Won't you, Dave?"

"Of course I will."

The technician picked up the saddle while Dave collected the man's bag from the floor. The three of them left the stable together and placed all the equipment in the technician's car.

They wandered back to their own car, and Dave asked, "Where to now, boss?"

"We try and track down Wesley Porter."

CHAPTER FIVE

The detached house set back from the road seemed as though it belonged on the pages of a magazine. The curved red-brick walls and its ornate wrought-iron gates hinted at what lay beyond. Dave opened the gates, to reveal the red-brick façade of a double-fronted house with a beautiful canopy porch above the bright-red front door.

"Well, this isn't too shabby," Dave announced as Kayli drew up outside the front door.

She noticed a sporty BMW sitting in the driveway, as well as a black Nissan Qashqai. "I think we're in luck. Can't say I'm looking forward to doing this."

"You'll be fine. I'm sure you're going to handle it in your own inimitable way."

Kayli turned and pulled a face at him. "Did you swallow a dictionary for breakfast this morning?"

He wrinkled his nose and poked out his tongue at her. "I can speak posh when the need arises."

Kayli chuckled and shook her head. "Whatever. Let's go."

They closed the car doors and crunched their way across the drive to the front door. A middle-aged man with slightly greying hair opened it soon after. "Hello. What do you want? This is private property. No hawkers allowed."

"Sorry to disturb you, Mr. Porter. We're DI Kayli Bright and DS Dave Chaplin from the Avon and Somerset Constabulary. Would it be possible to come in and have a brief chat with you?" Kayli flashed her warrant card for the man to study.

He appeared taken aback for a moment, sighed then stepped behind the door and allowed them into the house. "I was out in the back garden, tending to my wife's plants. What's this about?"

They followed him through the house and into the large garden that was mainly laid to lawn at the rear. He picked up the hosepipe and continued to water the pots full of flourishing Busy Lizzies that had recently blossomed in the fine weather they'd had in the past few weeks in between the heavy showers.

"We're sorry to disturb you, but we needed to ask you a few questions about your wife's death, if it's not too inconvenient."

He switched off the hosepipe and motioned for them to take a seat at the table on the patio under a large cream awning. "It's not inconvenient, but I must confess that I'm still feeling rather raw at present."

"I can imagine. I'm sorry for your loss. Perhaps you can tell us what you know about your wife's death?"

He frowned then rolled his eyes. "She died in hospital after falling off that damn horse of hers. What else do you need to know?"

"It's very sad. Were you at the hospital when she took her last breath?"

"Of course. The whole family were there. What are you getting at?"

"Nothing. I'm just ensuring all the facts are in place."

"In place...before what?"

Kayli felt cornered. During the drive over there, she had decided not to tell the husband they were treating his wife's death as suspicious until she had heard his version of the events. However, his sharp tongue and no-nonsense attitude were making her life difficult. "We have to carry out enquiries in all accidents of this nature, sir. I know how difficult this must be for you right now, but if you'll just answer our questions, we'll be out of your hair soon enough." She hoped the lie about investigating all accidents similar to Jessica's would make him calm enough to answer their questions without being too defensive.

"Very well. I wasn't aware that the police got involved in cases such as this, but ask your damn questions then leave me alone to grieve the loss of my dear wife."

"Thank you, sir. One question that has been bugging me is why you sold your wife's horse so soon after her death?"

He flung himself back in his chair and crossed one of his ankles over his over leg. "Someone been telling tales down at the stables, have they?"

"Not at all. Can you answer the question?"

He ground his teeth and glared at Kayli. "Why? Does it help with your investigation to know such trivial information?"

"It could prove to be an important fact in the case, sir."

He shook his head in apparent disbelief. "I was angry with the damn animal. If she hadn't been riding the bloody nag, then she'd still be alive today. Is that a good enough answer for you?"

"How did you manage to find a buyer so quickly, if you don't mind me asking?"

His foot dropped to the floor, and he sat forward in his chair. "A friend of mine had hinted over the years about how envious he was of Jess having the perfect horse. He confided in me that he'd be willing to pay a hefty sum if ever we considered selling it. I took him up on that offer the second Jess lost her life. The sooner the horse was off my hands, the better. I hated the damn thing even before her accident."

"May I ask why?" Kayli asked, thinking his reply a little strange.

"There are some things in this life that wind people up for no reason, Inspector. That horse was a personal thorn in my side. I can't explain it better than that."

"Was your daughter close to the horse? Did she agree to you selling it?"

"My daughter has no say in things that do not concern her. She doesn't know the horse has been sold yet. I'll tell her that in my own time, when I think she's over the grieving process and able to understand my reasoning behind doing what I've done."

Kayli couldn't help thinking that the man had gone out of his way to cause damage to his relationship with his daughter. "I hope that works out for you."

He tilted his head and narrowed his eyes. "What's that supposed to mean? That you think I've done the wrong thing?"

"I would have played things differently if I were in your shoes, yes. To each their own."

He rose from his chair in anger, and it toppled over behind him. "I want you to leave my house immediately. You weren't invited here, and I don't have to justify my actions to you or anybody else. Now get out!"

Kayli nudged Dave's leg, and they both remained seated. "Sit down, Mr. Porter. I haven't finished yet."

His angry gaze drifted between Kayli and Dave. "What else are you going to pick fault with?"

"I wasn't aware that I had. Please, sit down."

He reluctantly righted the chair and plonked into it. Folding his arms tightly across his heaving chest, he asked, "What else do you need to ask?"

"If your wife had any enemies."

His brow creased heavily. "Why?"

Kayli inhaled a deep breath. "Why? Because we believe your wife's accident was suspicious and we're treating her death as murder."

Kayli nearly jumped out of her skin when a deafening scream sounded behind her. She turned to see a teenager in a school uniform standing at the back door to the house. Her hands trembled as they covered her face. She began to sob uncontrollably.

Wesley shot out of his chair and rushed towards the girl. As he passed Kayli, he hissed through gritted teeth, "See what you've done now? Get out of my house before I throw you out."

"Dad, is it true?" the girl asked between sobs.

Wesley hugged his daughter and stroked her hair as he comforted her. "I doubt it, love. It's probably the police trying to pin something on someone that they've made up. They sink to such desperate levels all the time. You only have to read the newspapers to know that. They're leaving now."

Dave leaned over and whispered, "We better go. I doubt we're going to get anything out of him while he's in this mood."

Kayli nodded and left her seat. With sadness tugging at her heart, she walked towards the grieving father and daughter. It hadn't been her intention to upset anyone. She was only trying to seek justice for Jessica Porter. By the looks of things, her efforts had backfired considerably. She pulled out a business card and left it on the kitchen counter as she passed. "Ring me anytime if you think you need me. I'm sorry for your loss. We'll go back to the station and start the investigation into your wife's death. Sorry if the news I shared with you has upset you both. That truly wasn't my intention. If I could take the words back, I would. However, that wouldn't alter the facts. I'll be in touch soon if any evidence shows up regarding your wife's case."

With his daughter's head cushioned against his chest, Wesley glared and mouthed the words, "Just go."

Kayli and Dave left the house.

Once they were by the car, Dave let out a huge sigh. "Well, that went well—not!"

"Will you stop stating the obvious? It was a total fuck-up. I know that. There's no need for you to point out the error of my ways, Dave. Get in the car, and we'll discuss it en route to Amelia's house."

They both slipped into their seats. Kayli started the car and exited the drive before either of them spoke again.

"He seemed shocked to hear that his wife had been murdered," Dave suggested.

Kayli tapped her hands on the steering wheel. "To be honest with you, I'm not sure I could put a finger on how he reacted, as everything seemed to happen so quickly. Cathy's scream struck me like a bolt of lightning, shattered my nerves. If she hadn't shown up, I would have kept hounding Wesley until he broke down and gave us the answers we needed to begin our investigation. I found him rather defensive before his daughter arrived on the scene."

"I'm struggling to make head or tails of it. The man had a right to be defensive in my eyes. I think I would react the same way if a couple of coppers showed up at my house insinuating what we did."

"Really? That's where we differ, because I wouldn't. Of course I'd be shocked by the news, but then I would demand to know what the coppers investigating the incident were going to do about apprehending the suspect. Maybe that's my copper's brain functionality talking. Would I react the same way if I were just a member of the public?" Kayli shrugged. "I'm not sure." She slammed the heel of her hand into the steering wheel as her temper rose. "I'm wondering if I screwed up back there or if a genuine mistake happened and he jumped on the chance to kick us out. He'd already asked us to leave prior to that, remember?"

"I get what you're saying. Is it worth tying yourself up in knots to fathom that out?"

"I guess not. Let's see if we get a better result from her sister. We're not far now. I need to put on some music to calm me down. Hope you don't mind?"

"Go for it. I've got used to hearing that Luther Vandross crap over the past few months since your trip abroad."

Kayli chuckled and switched on the CD. "Something I learnt from the boys over there—when stress strikes, find something to calm yourself. I suppose I've latched on to music to help me do that. Just shove your fingers in your ears for the next ten minutes."

Dave grunted. Several minutes later, his leg jiggled up and down to the beat.

"See? It's not so bad after all, once you take the time to listen to his dulcet tones."

"I suppose so. Suranne likes his music, so I'm used to hearing it around the house. Some of his stuff is all right in small doses."

"Shame he died so young. Very talented man who is sorely missed."

"What is it with these musicians anyway? It's as if they strive hard to achieve the fame and notoriety but struggle to know what to do with it. The death toll rises every year of top singers and musicians dying at a relatively young age."

"It's very sad. A lot of them are marked as unexplained deaths, as well. I have a theory. Want to hear it?"

"Go on then, surprise me. I bet it's to do with drugs."

"That's where you'd be wrong, partner. My theory is that these people are afraid of getting old. They see clips of themselves when they first hit the top of the fame chart and crave for how they used to appear."

"Really? That sounds a little warped to me."

"Whatever. Some of them went under the knife regularly—you know, like Michael Jackson—but I sincerely believe that others just see their reflection in the mirror and hate the fact that age has crept up on them faster than they realise."

Dave sniggered. "I've never even considered that before. Not sure how I feel about your theory, if I'm honest."

"Ah, here we are. It passed the time if nothing else." Kayli grinned at him and exited the vehicle.

The property was an old Victorian house with bay windows and a white-rendered façade. Two front doors greeted them as they walked up the narrow front path. The garden was covered in grey slate with the odd ornamental grass scattered around for easy maintenance.

My kind of gardening, Kayli thought, admiring the effect. The right door had the name S Jameson written on a laminated piece of card on the letterbox while the other one had A Watson on it. Kayli rang the bell.

Within moments, a young blonde woman with sore-looking red eyes opened the door. "Hello? Can I help?"

Kayli and Dave flashed their IDs for her to examine. "DI Kayli Bright and DS Dave Chaplin of the Avon and Somerset Constabulary. Are you Amelia Watson?"

"I am. Have I done something wrong? I'm not aware of anything I might have done."

"No, not at all. We'd like a brief chat with you if it's all right. Mind if we come inside for a moment or two?"

"Okay. You'll have to excuse me. I'm not really with it as I've had a recent death in the family."

"We know. That's what our visit is concerning."

"It is. Oh right, I suppose that even simple accidents warrant investigation. Come through. I was just about to put the kettle on. Would you like a drink?"

"We'd love one please. Two coffees. One with one sugar and the other with two. Both white. Thanks very much."

The flat was quite large, and Amelia showed them through to a substantial kitchen diner that was light and airy at the rear of the property. They passed two other rooms on their journey. Because the doors were open, Kayli noted one of those rooms was a bedroom and the other was a smallish lounge. The kitchen seemed to be where Amelia spent most of her time, though. There were a couple of easy chairs close to the back door near the window that had a view of a large courtyard. Kayli looked around, admiring the woman's eye for furnishing her home. Pops of colour from the cushions and rugs scattered across the tiled floor contrasted nicely with the muted hues on the walls and brightened the room. It just felt comfortable and inviting, as if the house were willing to give everyone who entered a large hug.

Amelia filled the kettle and invited Kayli and Dave to sit opposite her on the stools at the island in the kitchen area while she prepared three mugs of coffee.

"How are you coping with your sister's death? If it's not a silly question?" Kayli asked.

"To be honest with you, it's a bit of a struggle. When we were all at the hospital standing vigil at her bedside before she passed away, I needed to be the strongest one there, to help the others through the ordeal. Since her death, I've spent most of the time crying. Actually, correct that, sobbing my heart out. I never thought I could miss someone so much in my life. It's devastating to think that person will never ring you or come and visit you anymore. I haven't had the heart to go round to see how my parents are coping, but they have each other for support now. It's a struggle to deal with this type of thing on your own. At least it is for me."

"There are places you can ring if you need to speak about your grief rather than bottling it up inside."

"I know. That type of thing has never appealed to me. Talking to strangers who are trained what to say. Who knows if they're truly listening to you? I know I would switch off if a person droned on and on about a loved one I didn't know from Adam. It might sound harsh, but I happen to think it's the truth. Anyway, how can I help *you*?"

The kettle finished boiling, and she poured the hot water into the mugs, added a drop of milk, and stirred the drinks before she handed them out.

"Thanks." Kayli accepted the mug and placed her hands around it as she prepared what to say next. "You should check them out if you find yourself struggling to cope. Either that, or perhaps go and stay with your parents for a few days until the pain eases a little. I think that's what I would do in the circumstances."

"I'll consider it. What do you need to know about Jess?" Her eyes filled up with tears when she mentioned her sister's name.

Kayli inhaled a large breath then let it out slowly. "There's no easy way to say this, but we believe your sister's death is suspicious."

Amelia gasped, and her eyes widened in fear. "What? Are you telling me that you think my sister was murdered? But how can that be when she fell off her horse?"

"We believe that her saddle was tampered with. The strap was cut. Her fall was unavoidable."

"But how do you know it was cut and didn't just break through wear and tear?"

"We've had it verified by a Scenes of Crime Officer at the stable, and he's taken the saddle away to examine it more thoroughly. I'm sorry to break the news to you like this. What I'm hoping you'll do is give us some form of clue where to go next with the investigation."

"What? How would I know what to do next?"

"We need possible names. People who you might think would want to harm your sister."

She shook her head slowly and puffed out her cheeks. "I'm not sure I can do that. This revelation has shocked me, if I'm honest with you. Why? Who could do such a thing to Jess? She was such a friendly, loveable person. Everyone I know adored her."

Kayli sighed. "I hate to ask this, but can you tell me what her marriage was like? It would be wonderful to get an insight into their marriage. Did she and Wesley get on as a couple?"

Amelia touched the side of her face. "Yes, as far as I know. They loved each other. Are you telling me that Wes is a suspect?"

"Not really, not unless we find anything out about him that we deem suspicious. How long have they been married?"

"Umm…let me think. Time flies by, as you can imagine. Cathy has just turned sixteen, and they got married as soon as Jess found out she was pregnant, so around sixteen years. They've always struck me as being the perfect couple."

"Okay, that's good to know." Kayli glanced sideways to check Dave was writing down the answers in his notebook before she asked her second question. "In that case, did Jess have any enemies that you can think of?"

Amelia's mouth turned down. "I can't think of anyone. As I've stated already, everyone loved Jess. She bent over backwards to be friendly to people. Didn't have a mean bone in her body. I really can't help you there."

"Please, I know how hard this must be, but try and think back. I'm not talking recently. Maybe something has happened in Jess's past that has reared its head in the last few weeks. Anything at all?"

Amelia clenched her hands together and stared at her mug as she thought. Slowly, she raised her eyes to look at Kayli and nodded. "Okay…when Jess came round here about a month ago, she was absolutely livid."

"Did she say what was irking her so much?"

"It was when she visited the stables. She'd noticed a slight graze on Nutmeg's neck. She asked around the yard, and someone took her to one side—don't ask me the name of that person, because I can't remember. Anyway, this person took her to one side and said that she'd seen Belinda strike Nutmeg. As you can imagine, Jess was furious. That horse means so much to her. Sorry, *meant* so much to her. She confronted this Belinda and told her never to go near Nutmeg again."

"We've been at the stables this morning, and I find it strange that no one bothered to mention the argument while we were down there. Make a note of that, Dave. We'll chase it up with the owner later."

"I don't want to get this woman in trouble. I'm just telling you what Jess told me."

"You won't be getting her in trouble. That's the type of information we need to hear in order to move the investigation forward. Do you know if Jess informed Susan Lord, the stable owner, of this?"

"I'm not sure. She didn't tell me that. Knowing how much she loved Nutmeg, I can't see Jess not saying anything to Susan."

"Another thing that has come to our attention that I'd like your take on is the fact that Wesley has sold the horse, barely a day after losing his wife. Were you aware of that?"

Amelia's mouth twisted in anger, and she glared at Kayli. "He's done what? Why? I can't believe he would do such a thing. I bet Cathy is beside herself."

"He's keeping the news from Cathy for the time being. Do you have any idea why he would do such a thing?"

"No clue whatsoever. I'm appalled by his actions and will be on the phone, voicing my opinion on the matter as soon as you leave. How could he? Jess adored that bloody horse. Surely he couldn't have been jealous of it, could he?"

"We're not sure. I think he's going more along the lines that he couldn't bear to have the horse around, knowing that the accident caused his wife's death."

"Does he know that you're treating the case as murder?" she asked, rubbing the side of her temple with her fingers as if she had a headache starting.

"He learnt about it at the end of the conversation. Sadly, Cathy overheard me telling her father. He was irate about that and asked us to leave. We'll give it a few days before we call back to see him."

"But surely Cathy wouldn't allow him to sell Nutmeg. She would have wanted to have held on to that horse because of the connection her mum had with it."

"Even though her father seems to blame the horse for Jess's death? Of course, we now know the horse wasn't to blame. He seemed pretty vehement that it was the right thing to do—get rid of it, I mean."

"But why so soon after Jess's death? I can't say it would be the first thing I thought about doing with all the arrangements he's going to have to deal with like her funeral et cetera. I don't know…I might be talking out of my arse there."

Kayli nodded. "I thought the same thing. Oops…you know what I mean."

"I'm at a loss to know why Wes would get rid of something so precious. Oh my, you don't think he's sold it for horsemeat, do you?"

Kayli gulped at the thought. "God, I hope not. Maybe we'll ask him to supply the name of the person he sold Nutmeg to the next time we question him. Once he's calmed down."

"I've not known him to be angry before. He always seemed a very placid type to me. I suppose he must have his faults like any other man on this earth. Otherwise, he'd still be married to his first wife, right?"

Kayli raised an inquisitive eyebrow. "Oh, I presumed that Jess was his first and only wife. Do you know his ex-wife?"

"I know of her. I've never had the privilege of meeting either her or their wayward son. Jess told me that Wes refused to contact either of them because the boy—Patrick, I believe his name is—had become unruly, and his behaviour was causing friction between Cordelia—she's his ex-wife—and Wes. He blamed her for the way the boy had turned out."

"Does Cordelia live in the area?"

"Not far, but I'm not sure where. I think 'far enough away not to be a problem' was how Jess put it to me."

"Okay, we'll look into that back at the station. Any idea what sort of mischief the son has got up to in the past?"

"Usual teenage stuff, I presume. I think he was arrested for stealing a car with a group of his mates when he was fourteen or fifteen."

"I see. How old is he now?"

"Roughly about sixteen or seventeen."

"Did Jess meet Wes while he was still married to his ex?"

"No. He'd split up with her the month before. They fell in love and became pregnant with Cathy within a couple of months of their first date. His divorce came through one day, and they got married at the registry office the next."

"Why the rush, apart from the fact that Jess was pregnant?"

"They both said they couldn't wait to be husband and wife, and with the baby due in a few months, they were eager to begin their married life and start looking for a nice place to live." In spite of coming across as holding it together, Amelia paused and wiped a stray tear from the corner of her eye with a tissue. "I'm sorry. The grief hits me in waves when I least expect it. I suppose it's going to be a darn sight worse now I know that she was murdered. My God, are you sure you couldn't have made a mistake? It's so hard to digest. Why Jess? She was such a beautiful person."

"I'm sorry. At this moment in time, there is very little doubt in my mind that this is a murder enquiry. I understand what you must be going through, but it's really important for us to ascertain if Jess had any people with any gripes against her. Wes wasn't very forthcoming when we visited him, so anything you can give us at this time will help the investigation."

"I'll do my best, if you're willing to give me some time to push past the grief."

"Take all the time you need. Sorry to keep harping on about their marriage, but I'm wondering if Jess ever voiced any concerns regarding it. Did she ever have any doubts about it or Wes?"

Amelia sniffled and shook her head. "No. At least I can't think of any time she regretted her decision to marry Wes so quickly. As far as I know, they loved each other very much."

"What about before Wes came on the scene? Jess was a very attractive lady. She must have had other boyfriends."

"Oh, she did. The list would be endless, and I'm not sure I could name all of them now, not after all this time."

Kayli smiled. "Sorry to pressure you, but would you try?"

She fell quiet for a few moments, narrowing her eyes as she thought. "She went out with a guy for a couple of years before she met Wes. He was called Stuart Collins. Immediately before that, I think she went out with a Bruce Dyer. I'm sorry, but I don't have their addresses or anything else that will help. I'm hoping that I've remembered their names properly."

"We'll do some digging, so don't worry. What about ex-girlfriends Jess might have fallen out with? Or am I barking up the wrong tree there?"

Her eyes narrowed again. "Actually... Jess used to be best friends with a woman named Deanne Mitchell, but their relationship turned nasty when Deanne had a miscarriage. She was depressed a lot of the time. Jess used to go round there frequently to ensure she was all right. I seem to remember that one day Deanne had nipped out to the supermarket, and when she came home, she found Jess in the lounge talking to her boyfriend. Deanne flew off the handle and accused them of having an affair. Jess was gobsmacked by the way Deanne treated her. She walked out of there with scratches all over her face and arms. She told me that Deanne just lost it. Even kicked her boyfriend out of the house that very day."

"Did Jess ever get in contact with this Deanne again?"

71

"I don't think so. Deanne made herself perfectly clear that she wanted nothing more to do with either of them, which suited Jess."

Kayli tilted her head. "So you never really got to the bottom of why Deanne lost it with Jess?"

"Not really. Although Jess seemed to think it was hormone related—you know, Deanne losing the baby like that. I just think the woman used the incident as an excuse to kick her boyfriend out."

"Are you saying that you think they weren't getting along?"

"I don't know the ins and outs, but I think the pregnancy was unexpected, and the boyfriend wasn't too impressed when he heard the news. I think it put a lot of strain on their relationship. There was no reason for Deanne to take it out on Jess the way she did, though. That was just spiteful."

"So Jess steered clear of this Deanne after that happened?"

Amelia appeared to mull the question over again before she answered, "I believe so. My sister was a lot like me in that respect—once someone does something as obscure as striking out then there really is no way back."

"Do you have an address for Deanne? Sorry, when did this incident take place? Can you remember?"

She shrugged. "At least a couple of years ago. Sorry, no idea what her address is or was. I was appalled by her behaviour. I even urged Jess to contact the police about the incident. The woman assaulted her, for goodness' sake, but Jess wouldn't do it. She told me she didn't intend on ever seeing Deanne again so she was willing to let it go."

"Can you remember what the boyfriend's name was?"

"Don't quote me on this, but I think it was Alan. I haven't got a clue what his surname is."

"We'll try and make a connection with him and Deanne back at the station. That's really helpful. Anyone else?"

"Hang on…yes, I forgot to add Carl Longhurst to the list of ex-boyfriends. Jess mentioned him in passing recently. She told me that she'd seen him in town a few weeks ago. He'd left the country to work in Denmark long before Jessica met Wes. Anyway, she said it was nice to see him after all these years, and they'd had a coffee in town."

"Is Wes aware of their meeting?"

"I don't know, to tell you the truth. I thought Jess was going to marry Carl at one point. Maybe that's why he took off. Perhaps the thought of settling down at such a young age scared the crap out of him."

"We'll ask the question if we ever catch up with him. Did Jess work?"

"No, she used to be a PA for a businessman in the city until she fell pregnant. Wes encouraged her to give up work early so that she could look after the baby before Cathy was born and after, which I thought was quite sweet."

"Why was that so important to Wes, do you think?"

"Because back then, he used to run a nightclub, and he hated the thought of not seeing Jess, what with them working opposite shifts."

Kayli nodded, totally understanding. "And Jess was up for that? Sitting at home all day, waiting for the baby to pop out?"

"Yes, it wasn't for long anyway as Wes decided to jack the night-club life in and tried to find a job with more suitable hours before the baby came along. That's when he spotted an ad in the paper of some-one selling a steam-cleaning business. He started off with just a steam cleaner. He used to go round to different people's houses—it proved to be very popular, and he soon diversified after a few months. He began searching for commercial premises where he could offer the full valeting service to his customers. He employed immigrants—not illegal ones as far as I know—and turned a small car-cleaning company into a huge money-spinner."

"Looking at their house, it's in a good area and appeared to have undergone some recent renovations."

"It's a newbuild. Jess contributed to the house so they could move up the ladder. Our grandmother left a decent sum in her will for each of us. I bought this place. Up until then, I was still living at home with Mum and Dad. Jess decided to put her inheritance towards the new house. Wes was in total agreement with that. He would have been foolish to have turned down the offer."

"Has Jess always been self-sufficient throughout the marriage?"

"She was always good at saving her money, if that's what you're asking? She's savvy with money in that she doesn't waste it on frivolous things. I suppose some would even call her tight because she used to write down the meter readings at the end of each month and tot up how much they were spending on the gas and electric."

"Any reason she did that?"

"None as far as I know. Not sure where she picked up the habit from. Neither Mum nor Dad have ever watched the pennies as closely as she used to. I was quite surprised when she told me how much she was putting in the pot towards the new home."

"May I ask how much?" Kayli tilted her head.

"Over a hundred grand. She even landscaped the garden. She was delighted with the result and chuffed to bits with the building firm they chose to carry out the work."

"Do you know which firm she used?"

"Matt Fletcher is the builder's name, but I can't tell you the name of the firm. He's local anyway, so it shouldn't be that difficult to find him."

"Excellent news. Thanks for that. How are your parents coping?"

"They're beside themselves. They'll be a darn sight worse once they hear that Jess was murdered. I still can't believe it myself."

"It must have been a shock to lose her like that. In the hospital, I mean. I'll need to speak to them in the next few days. I don't want to disturb them now, though."

"I'll let them know. Do you want me to tell them that you're conducting a murder enquiry?"

"If you think it'll be better coming from you."

"I think it will. I'll nip round there and tell them later."

"What about Wes's parents? Are they still alive?"

"His father died a few years ago, liver cancer. However, his mum lives in sheltered housing not far from here."

"Okay. I think we've covered everything now, unless there's anything else you think we should know."

She shook her head. "No, I don't think so. Perhaps you should leave a card in case I remember anything once you leave and my head is a little clearer."

"I was about to suggest the same." Kayli slid a business card across the work surface. "Again, I'm sorry for your loss and for having to break the unsavoury news to you. I want to assure you, though, that we'll do everything we can to find the person responsible for stripping your sister of her life."

The three of them left their seats and walked towards the front door. On the way, Kayli's heart squeezed when she saw a photo on the wall of the two sisters laughing together. *Jess, who killed you? What secrets am I about to uncover?*

CHAPTER SIX

Kayli was contemplative during the journey back to the station, prompting Dave to ask if she was okay. "I'm fine. Just wondering what we're going to uncover in this case, if anything. Why would anyone purposefully set out to kill Jess? Did you see the photo of her with her sister? She seemed such a jolly person, so full of life, and yet now, she's lying in the cold store cabinet at the mortuary, awaiting her funeral. There really doesn't seem to be any justice in the world when an innocent life such as hers is lost."

"I'll second that. What's your take on what we've heard so far? I mean, who is top of your suspect list?"

"I knew what you were getting at. Honestly? I'm torn at the moment. Until we do more digging, I don't think the pieces will slot into place anytime soon. I don't want to sit back on this case. I want whoever did this to Jess to be punished sooner rather than later. I'm guessing that person is unhinged in some way."

"Unhinged?" Dave replied, turning to face her.

"They'd have to be to kill someone as nice as Jess. No one has said a bad word against her yet, right?"

"I suppose."

"Okay, consider it another way, her death was intentional, pre-meditated even. It takes an evil mind to carry out something as bad as that. We need to find that person before they repeat the process."

"I'm with you. But where do we start looking?"

"It's almost five-thirty now. We'll see what the others have found while we've been out and then call it a day. We'll recap everything with the others first thing, when our brains are fresher."

"Knowing you, you'll be tossing and turning all night, trying to figure it out before we have that discussion."

She smiled. "You know me so well. Doesn't a case ever grab you by the throat, Dave?"

"Nope! I'm quite happy sitting back and letting you deal with all the angst. That's why you're a DI and I'm a DS."

"Coward. If ever you feel like changing your mind about that, I'd willingly put your name forward for promotion."

"Ha! And there was me thinking you enjoyed working alongside me."

Kayli tutted. "Don't twist my bloody words. That's not what I was saying, and you damn well know it." She thumped him in the thigh then parked in the station car park.

"I know. You'd miss my startling wit and amazing powers of deduction."

Kayli stared at him, her mouth hanging open.

"God, I never knew you had so many fillings," he said, tearing open the door and scrambling out of the car before she clouted him.

Kayli leaned over and pointed. "I'll get you for that."

They walked through the reception area together, past several young men slouching in the chairs along one side of the room. Kayli motioned with her head towards the men and mouthed to the desk sergeant if everything was okay. Ray nodded. Kayli and Dave continued up the stairs to the incident room and found DCI Davis waiting at the top of the stairs.

"Ah, just the person I wanted to see. Do you have a moment, Inspector?"

"I do. You go ahead, Dave. I'll catch up with you."

Dave smiled and nodded then he disappeared into the incident room.

"Anything wrong, ma'am?" Kayli asked, an uneasy feeling niggling at her stomach.

"No. Why do you always act as though you've done something wrong? All I wanted to ask was how the case is going. My take is it'll be a tricky one, I bet."

"I can neither deny or confirm that. It's just too early, ma'am. I think we have a strong list of suspects to trawl through in the morning before the investigation begins in earnest. Sad that Jess lost her life so young. She was well-liked by everyone we've interviewed so far."

"And what about the husband? Is he in the frame for this, Kayli?"

"I'm not confident either way after dealing with him today. His actions to date have been questionable. That could be down to his grief or something more sinister being afoot. I've decided to hold back any suspicions attempting to rear their head in his direction for now."

"I'll leave it in your capable hands. Give me a shout if you need to run anything past me."

"I will, ma'am. I'll be calling it a day soon."

"Me, too. Any plans for this evening?"

"I'll take some paperwork home with me to keep me company as Mark starts work at eight."

She patted Kayli on the arm and offered her a sympathetic smile. "That must be tough to deal with."

"I get waves of thinking it's okay and others where all I want to do is snuggle up with him and forget the world we live in. I could do with a snuggle after the day I've had, but it ain't gonna happen, and we've got to deal with it."

"Surely there has to be a more suitable job out there for him to consider?"

"We appear to spend most of our time together scouring the situations vacant in the local newspaper. Nothing jumps out, though. He loves the job. It's the time apart we're both struggling with." Trying to remain upbeat about a situation she was eager to alter, she added, "I'm sure things will get better soon."

"I hope things work out for you both. Not an ideal situation to find yourselves in given that you're newlyweds. Enjoy your evening. Don't work too hard."

"Thanks. You, too, ma'am." Kayli watched the DCI walk down the stairs then turned to enter the incident room. She found Dave sitting at his desk, leaning back with his hands on his head, while Donna filled him in on what was written in her notes. "Hey, wait for me. What have you found out, Donna?"

"Sorry, boss. Dave was getting antsy with me, impatient bugger."

"You don't have to tell me what he's like. I see enough of his bad traits when we're out and about together."

"Hey, when you two have quite finished talking about me as if I wasn't in the room, can we get back to business?"

Kayli chuckled. "Go on then. What have you found out about the owner and the stables, Donna?"

"To be honest, boss, very little."

"That's disappointing but also good in the respect that we needn't waste any extra time investigating that route. So are you telling me that no other accidents along this line have been reported down there?"

"Nothing in our system. Susan Lord has a clean sheet, too."

"Good. Okay. Dave, did you bring the CCTV discs in?"

"I did. Graeme has agreed to look over them in the morning, if that's okay?"

Kayli nodded. "I agree. I've had enough for one day, let's start afresh in the morning."

The team packed up their things and left together.

~ ~ ~

Around thirty minutes later, Kayli walked through the front door of her small semi to the tempting smell of sausages wafting into the lounge from the kitchen. She slipped off her shoes and snuck up behind her husband, who was standing at the stove. He turned around, and they shared a long kiss.

"What's for dinner, apart from sausages?"

"SPO, as my old nan used to call it. Only in this case, it would be SPOB."

Kayli laughed and leaned over to see what was going on behind him. Sausages and onions sizzled in a frying pan. Potatoes boiled in one pot whilst baked beans cooked in another. "S is for the sausages. P for the potatoes. O is for onions. Right?"

"Give the girl a gold star! And to bring the dish together, it should always be served with baked beans—at least when I cook it. My old gran would probably turn in her grave if she knew I'd added that to her recipe."

"I doubt it. She'd be super proud of you for looking after your wife so well."

He pecked her on the nose then laughed. "That's the best thing I love about you."

"What's that?"

"You're easily pleased."

"Hey, I appreciate you taking the time out of your day to prepare and cook my meals. It really means a lot. I don't know many men who would do that for their wives."

"It's a partnership, love. If I was still in the army, I doubt I would have the time to tinker in the kitchen. What else am I going to do all day?"

"They broke the mould when you were born. I'm eternally grateful for your input in our marriage."

"Stop with the mushiness. Are you hungry?"

"You bet. Dave and I were so busy interviewing people today that we missed out on lunch. Damn, he didn't remind me, either. I owe him an apology in the morning."

"I'll give you an extra sausage and double helping of mash in that case."

Kayli opened the cutlery drawer and extracted the knives and forks to lay the table. "Normal portion for me, thanks."

Mark tutted. She knew what was coming next.

"You still haven't put those pounds back on that you lost a few months ago."

"I know. I like my weight the way it is. It serves as a reminder of how close I came to losing you."

"I've heard it all now. Your logic beggars belief at times. Here you go. Tuck in."

Kayli sat at the table and squirted her meal with ketchup. Her tummy rumbled, eager for the contents of her plate. "This is yummy," she said, nibbling on the herby Cumberland sausage.

"Glad you think so. How has your day been? Save the gruesome details until after dinner."

"It's been a day of interviewing people. No gruesome details to divulge on this one. What we have uncovered is a lot of heartache. A woman's death from an accident has now been established as murder. Dave and I received a tipoff this morning from someone working at the stables where the woman used to keep her horse, and we had to go out and break the news to her family." She placed a large forkful of buttery mash in her mouth.

"How awful. Why the change of heart on the case?"

"We found that her saddle had been tampered with. A strap has been cut intentionally."

"No chance it could have worn over time?"

"Nope, not according to the forensic technician anyway."

"That's terrible. So someone deliberately did it with the intention of people thinking it was an accident. Did she fall off her horse?"

"Yep, not only that, she fell backwards over a large tree trunk. There was no way she could have avoided breaking her back in the fall."

"Ouch! Painful."

"She died in hospital from internal injuries the day before yesterday. We received a call from the person in charge of tidying up the stable she used."

"That poor woman. I don't envy you trying to figure out who did it. Any clues at this early stage?"

"Not really. Her husband was a tad off with Dave and me when we showed up at the house."

"To be expected if he's grieving, love."

"I know. I'm prepared to give him the benefit of the doubt for now at least. Enough about my boring day. What have you been up to?"

"If you think your day was boring, my day would have driven you to distraction. I managed to sort out the gas and electric with a cheaper supplier. That in itself was a great achievement on my part."

"Excellent news. How much did you manage to save us?"

"They reckon three hundred and twenty quid. It'll go towards our holiday in the summer, if you're still up for it?"

"You bet. Fancy going to one of the Greek islands? I've never been but I've heard they're all pretty special."

"I'm easy. You choose, and I'll tag along for the ride."

"In other words, if the place I choose turns out to be a dive, I'll get the blame, right?" He gave her a cheeky wink and shovelled beans in his mouth.

"What time do you have to leave?" she asked.

"Around ten to eight, so not for a while yet."

"Good. We'll leave the washing up. I can do that after you've gone. I'm in need of a cuddle."

"If you insist. Are you sure you're okay?"

"Fine, except that I miss you when you're not around."

"I know. Think of the money!"

"If it wasn't necessary to have money coming in, I'd say jack your job in tomorrow."

Mark finished his meal, pushed his plate away, and sighed. "We've been over this a number of times, love."

"I know. Just ignore me. I suppose today's shenanigans highlighted how short life can be and how much we should appreciate those around us more."

"I know what you're saying. I'm sure things will work out for the best."

They left the plates on the table and took their coffees through to the lounge. Kayli turned on the news, and with mixed feelings, she watched the story of her case unfold, unsure how the press had got wind of the investigation so quickly. There was no way any of her team would have discussed it with the media folks without informing her first. She made a mental note to ring the TV station in the morning to find out who had given them the facts. She had a sneaking suspicion Wes was behind it.

"Everything all right? You've gone quiet."

"Yep, just listening to the report. It's pretty damn accurate, considering I haven't shared any facts with the media yet."

"That could be a problem, yes?"

"Maybe, maybe not. Makes you wonder if the murderer has leaked the story intentionally."

"Why?"

Kayli shrugged. "Haven't got a clue, but I intend to find out tomorrow. I'll put it to the top of my to-do list."

"There's such a lot for you to contend with in your job. It seems nothing ever goes according to plan."

"Exactly. Never mind, I'm sure I'll be able to sort it in the morning. Fancy some ice cream before you go?"

"You've twisted my arm. I bought a new flavour the other day if you want to start on that one. Salted caramel."

"Sounds lush. I'll be back in a second." She dished up a couple of scoopfuls each and returned to the lounge.

"So which direction will your case go in now?" Mark asked, wincing when the cold of the ice cream hit his teeth.

"We've got a few angles to discuss with the team tomorrow and the CCTV footage from the stables to study before we do anything else."

"I have every faith in you. Right, I better eat this and shift my arse into gear, otherwise I'll get too comfortable and want to stay here all evening."

"You could always pull a sickie."

He chuckled. "You always say that. The day you pull one is the day I do it."

Kayli curled her lip. "Ain't gonna happen, is it?"

"Not anytime soon." He kissed her, placed his bowl on the coffee table, and shot upstairs to get changed.

Kayli almost swooned when he walked into the room, wearing his dinner jacket and bow tie. She admired him in the suit then felt sad it wasn't for her benefit. The feeling turned to anger at the thought of the young women he would meet that evening, who would no doubt be fawning all over him. She had never been the jealous type before so she kept her emotions well hidden from Mark. If he ever found out how she felt, he would hit the roof. He'd never given her any reason to cause her to doubt his faithfulness. She felt ashamed when the jealousy bug struck. "You look handsome, as usual. Hope the girls manage to keep their hands to themselves tonight."

"They will. I'll make sure of that. There's only one girl I'm interested in, and I know exactly where she'll be—tucked up in bed, waiting for me to come home to her."

Kayli chuckled. "You old charmer. Some might say you have me on a ball and chain. Not me, of course."

He roared with laughter. "And that picture will remain in my head all evening now, so thanks for that. I love you, sweetheart. Have a good evening. I better skedaddle."

"Take care. Ring me if you get the chance."

"I will. Have fun slaving over your paperwork."

He kissed her goodbye, and before he'd even closed the front door, a twinge pulling at her heart. Kayli made herself another coffee, went upstairs to put on her PJs, then sat down to tackle the paperwork she'd brought home.

During the chore, all she could think about was the way Cathy and her father had reacted to the news that Jessica Porter had been murdered. *Is it too soon to return and question him?* She deliberated the question for the next few hours. Around the time she was due to go to bed, she decided it was too soon and that it would be best to leave it until the family had buried Jess before she bombarded them with more questions.

CHAPTER SEVEN

Kayli struggled out of bed the next morning, tired because her mind had refused to shut down. She'd still been awake when Mark arrived home at three-thirty.

"Are you going to be all right at work today?" he mumbled, still half-asleep.

She yawned and withdrew her navy skirt suit from the wardrobe. "I'm going to have to be. Go back to sleep. There's no point both of us being exhausted. I'll get dressed in the spare room. See you this evening, love."

"Don't I get a kiss before you go?" he asked sleepily.

Kayli smiled and crossed the room to peck him on the cheek. He had already fallen asleep. "Goodnight, sleepyhead."

She dressed and was out the door within twenty minutes. After depositing the paperwork she'd taken home with her the night before in the office, she bought herself a coffee and walked over to the whiteboard, where she jotted down the main facts she and Dave had accrued the previous day.

Dave entered the room around ten minutes later. "Morning, boss. How long have you been here?"

"A few hours," she replied, hoping to spark a reaction from him. She laughed as his eyes widened to the size of beachballs. "I'm joking. Only ten minutes, give or take. Thought I'd make an early start on getting the facts down on the board before you guys showed up, then we can get down to business ASAP."

"Good idea. Anything I can do?"

She grinned at him. "Apart from top up my coffee cup, not a lot."

Dave rolled his eyes. "On it now." As he made his way over to the vending machine, he called out, "Looks like you had a rough night. Not meaning any disrespect."

"Astute, as always, partner. I had a crap night. This case is in danger of getting under my skin. Couldn't stop thinking about Jess all night. I was still wide awake when Mark came home halfway through the night."

"Ouch. That bad, eh?" he said, handing her a cup of coffee.

"Did you see the news last night?"

Dave shook his head. "No. What did I miss?"

"Our case mainly. I'm going to ring the station this morning to find out who gave them the authority to run the story."

"Who do you think it was?"

"My inkling is Wesley Porter. I'd prefer to be proved wrong on that notion, however. The other task I think we should do first thing is view the CCTV footage. Can you do that with Graeme for me?"

"Of course. What's the betting that nothing shows up?"

"I'm thinking you'll be wrong about that. Want to put your money where your mouth is?"

Dave nodded.

"If nothing comes to light, I buy lunch for the team. If something shows up, lunch is on you. Deal?"

"If I have to. You must be pretty sure something is going to turn up."

"I am. At least I'm hopeful."

Donna and Graeme walked through the door.

"Morning, guys. I think lunch will be on Dave today," Kayli added with a wink at her partner. "Get yourselves a drink and gather around, if you will."

They spent the next fifteen minutes going over the evidence and clues they had so far. As she spoke, Kayli added the names to the list of suspects on the board.

"Who's your money on at this point, boss?" Graeme asked.

"Honestly? I'm torn at present. One minute, I think the husband is to blame, and the next…well, I haven't quite decided who else can possibly be in the frame so far. Donna, I'm counting on you to work your magic and find something during the background checks of these people." Kayli pointed at the list of suspects on the board—the three of Jess's former boyfriends and three females Jess had reasons to possibly have fallen out with in recent months. One of those people was Cordelia Porter, Wes's ex-wife.

"But the husband is going to continue to be our main suspect. Is that what you're saying?" Dave queried.

"I'm in two minds about that. Let's leave things as they are at present. Right, we've all got our different jobs to do. Let's crack on and reassemble at…say…eleven? To bring everyone up-to-date on what we've uncovered."

The team all agreed and returned to their desks to begin their tasks while Kayli headed for her office. She noted the time on her watch—it was ten minutes to nine—and she decided to look through the post that had appeared overnight. At bang on nine, she rang her contact at the television station. "Hi, Gordon. It's Kayli Bright. I realise how busy you might be, but if you can spare me five minutes for a chat, I'd appreciate it."

"Of course I can spare the time. What's up, Kayli?"

"You ran a story on the evening news bulletin last night about the woman who lost her life after falling off her horse."

"I know the one you're referring to. Tragic case. Don't tell me you're dealing with it?"

"I am. May I ask where you got your information from?"

"From the horse's mouth, you could say. The husband rang and asked us to run the story in the hope we might help the police catch the killer."

Kayli blew out a breath. "And you didn't think to check the story out before running it, Gordon?"

"To tell you the truth, I was torn but then thought it was too good an opportunity to miss out on, knowing what some of the nationals are like. They would've pounced on the story if I'd neglected to air it."

"How many stories of this type come your way?"

"I'm sorry. I'm not with you."

"You know, where a member of the public contacts you rather than the police regarding a major crime. Do you get where I'm coming from now?"

He gasped. "Reading between the lines, I'd say you're telling me that you think the husband has something to do with her murder."

"Whoa, steady on there. I didn't say that. What I'm trying to ascertain is that if a major crime occurs in the area, how do you usually hear about that crime?"

"Ah, I'm with you. Generally, through you guys. Are you telling me off for running the story, Kayli?"

"Not exactly. I do think you're very remiss for not checking the facts out first before you aired it, given where the story came from."

"Damn. In my haste for getting the story out there before the big boys cashed in on it, I've screwed up, right?"

"I wouldn't necessarily put it that way, but maybe if you'd taken a step back and thought it through, you would have realised your mistake. As the investigating officer, I would have come to you for help, as I always do, once my team and I have decided which way the case was going. All you've succeeded in doing is tipping a possible murderer off in your haste to be top dog."

He exhaled a large breath. "I've royally fucked up, haven't I? Jesus, will you ever trust me again?"

In spite of the gravity of the situation, she couldn't help but chuckle. "Of course I will. All I'm asking is that if a situation like this crops up in the future, you think it through thoroughly and dig around for who is leading the case. We value the exposure you guys give us during a case. It's important that we maintain a healthy relationship with the media. Things like this can cause a lot of damage going forward."

"God, I'm such a prick. You know it's totally out of character for me. To be truthful with you, I felt sorry for the bloke. That was another major contribution to me running the story. I kind of put myself in his shoes for a moment."

"I appreciate what you're getting at. All I'm saying is take a step back. Between you and me, the guy has done a few things that are a little obscure for someone who is supposed to be grieving. I know we all grieve differently. Maybe that's why I can't get my head around the decisions he's taken in the last few days."

"Care to share what you're referring to?"

Kayli smiled and shook her head. "Nice try, Gordon. All I'm advising is that you take a step back in the future and assess the situation before thinking how wonderful it would be to be the first to air a major story."

"Honestly, I appreciate the way you've slapped my wrist so gently instead of pulling me across red-hot coals. I promise you that I will never put myself in this situation again."

"That's reassuring to know. Out of curiosity, can I ask what type of reaction you've had from the general public since you aired the story?"

"The phones have been nonstop here. There's definitely a lot of interest surrounding this case."

"Thanks. Okay, I better get on and try and catch myself a killer before the general public try and muscle in on the act."

"Ouch, that was below the belt, even for you, Kayli."

"Shit happens, as they say, Gordon. Thanks for speaking to me."

"Always happy to oblige. You know that. Hope you find who you're searching for soon."

"So do I. Speak soon." Kayli ended the call as she always liked to with those she regarded as influential—on a good note. She sat back in her chair, contemplating the conversation she'd just had with a man she'd known professionally for quite a few years. She couldn't really blame him for chomping at the bit the way he had. She just hoped that his eagerness didn't prove to be too detrimental to the case.

Dave burst into the room. "You need to see this, boss."

He rushed out again, and Kayli shot out of her chair and chased after him. She found Dave looking over Graeme's shoulder. "What have you uncovered?"

He motioned to the grainy picture on the screen. "Watch. Play it, Graeme."

Graeme hit a button on the keyboard, and the image sprang to life before their eyes.

"Is this the person? Stupid question. Ignore that. Who else would dress all in black and be there in the dead of night? How did the person get in?"

"This is the camera at the gate. The person climbed up the gate and jumped down the other side to gain entry."

"Can you tell if the person is male or female by the way they move?"

"My take is that they're male, but don't quote me on that," her partner stated.

"Damn, he or she has gone off camera. Do any of the other cameras pick them up?"

"We're still working on that. I just thought you'd want to know what we'd stumbled across first."

Kayli patted Graeme on the shoulder. "Do your best to find out what they did next."

"I will."

Kayli walked over to Donna, who was concentrating on the screen ahead of her so much that she jumped when Kayli spoke to her.

"Everything all right, Donna?"

"You frightened the life out of me, boss. I think so. Early days yet, and there are a few people to go through, but I've found several things that you'll be interested in. Nothing major at this point, though."

"I'm all ears." Kayli sat beside her.

Donna withdrew her gaze from the screen and looked down at her notes. "I've mainly been searching things related to the ex-boyfriends. Carl Longhurst has recently returned from Denmark and bought a flat in the area. I've written down his address for you."

"Excellent news. Dave and I can interview him in the next day or two. Have you discovered anything unsavoury about him?"

"Not really, boss. I'm delving into his work record now. It's proving a little difficult only because his last job was abroad. I'll keep digging on that."

"Do your best. What about the other two exes?"

"Stuart Collins works at a hotel in the area as a pastry chef. Haven't found anything untoward hidden in his background to be concerned about. Bruce Dyer is a different matter entirely. I suppose I would class him as a petty criminal. He's been in and out of prison for years."

"Has he now? On what charges?"

"Anything from pickpocketing and robbery to the odd ABH charge."

"Actual Bodily Harm? That's an interesting aspect. Who was it against?"

"An ex-girlfriend, by all accounts. He showed up at her door, asking for money for a drug habit he'd developed on the inside, and punched her a few times in the head when she refused to give him any."

"Sounds like a pleasant chap and someone I'm keen to chat with. Note down his address for me, will you? Does he work?"

"Not that I can tell. He's coming up on the system as drawing benefits."

"Anything else?"

"Not really as yet. I'm just looking into the female names you listed. I'll get back to you when I find anything of use."

Kayli smiled and rose from her chair. "Thanks, Donna. Good luck." She walked back to Graeme's desk as he and Dave spotted something else on the screen. "What have you found?"

Dave pointed to the very edge of the screen. "This is the camera in the courtyard. I might be wrong but I'm guessing that stall is where Nutmeg was kept."

Kayli peered at the screen to get her bearings and slowly nodded. "I think you're right. So the person entered the stall and emerged when?"

They watched the screen and Kayli noted the time on the top left of the monitor.

"There!" Dave pointed again. "They were in and out within five minutes."

Kayli perched on the desk behind her. "Damn, is that all it takes to end a bloody life? Five crappy minutes?" She placed a hand on her forehead and closed her eyes when the start of a headache came on.

"Are you all right?" Dave asked.

"Yeah, I'll be fine. Eager for lunchtime, especially as I skipped breakfast and you'll be buying lunch. I was thinking along the lines of fish and chips. How expandable is your wallet, DS Chaplin?"

"What? You're having a laugh, aren't you?" he asked, clearly flabbergasted.

She dropped her hand from her temple and laughed. "Yes, I wouldn't do that to you. A roll or sandwich from the local deli will suffice."

"Bloody hell! I was thinking along the lines more of a bag of crisps and an apple. You know, the type of thing my mum used to send me off to school with all those years ago."

"Nice try, matey. I know damn well your mother wouldn't have treated you so poorly, and shame on you for suggesting otherwise. Right. Enough of this frivolity. Dave, you and I need to get on the road. I want to head back to the stables, have a word with Susan and this Belinda Moss, who has come to our attention. Donna, can you make the background checks on those two a priority and get back to me via my mobile if anything shows up?"

"I'll start now, boss."

~ ~ ~

Kayli pulled her vehicle to a standstill in the stable's car park under the gaze of several people. Some were employees, and others were owners intending to ride their horses, judging by the way they were dressed.

"We appear to be of interest to some folks," Dave said as he and Kayli left the car and walked towards Susan's office.

"So it would seem. Let's not read anything sinister into that just yet, partner. Although I have to say the hairs on the back of my neck are standing up right now, being back here."

"Glad I'm not alone."

Kayli smiled and pushed open the door to the office.

Susan glanced up immediately and left her seat. "Hello there. To what do we owe the pleasure so soon after your last trip?"

Kayli produced the CCTV disc, which Graeme had copied, and handed it to Susan. "Can you place that in your machine? We have something to show you."

Susan's hand shook when she grasped the disc.

"That sounds mighty ominous. The machine is over here."

They followed Susan through the reception area towards her desk at the rear where she placed the disc in the machine and press the button on the TV screen. Once the screen had warmed up, she hit the 'play' button on the machine and stood back a little so all three of them could view what was going on.

As soon as the figure scaled the gates, Susan gasped. "What the hell?" Do you know who this person is?"

Kayli shrugged. "We were kind of hoping you'd be able to tell us that."

Susan paused the CD player, placed her hand on her chest, and asked in disbelief, "Me? How in God's name would I know who it is?"

"Call it wishful thinking on our part. Keep the disc running. There's more."

Susan sighed and hit the 'play' button a second time. The figure searched for the right stable then disappeared inside, only to reappear five minutes later and close the half-stable door before leaving the way they had entered.

"My God, what are you showing me? That this person broke into my property and caused Jess's accident?"

"That's how we're reading things, yes."

"Crap, I need to get this place secured properly. I'll stop the bastards from coming in that way. I'll order some barbed wire immediately. Crikey! What else can I say other than that? I'm mortified beyond belief. I genuinely thought you were clutching at straws when you said you were investigating Jess's murder. How wrong could I be? My God, to think this despicable person carried out their deplorable deed on my premises…well, I'm appalled and ashamed by this."

"As are we. First of all, I wouldn't advice the use of barbed wire. You're liable to be sued by someone if they hurt themselves. Not sure what to suggest other than you should seek the advice of someone in security perhaps. Secondly, I need you to take a good look at the person's build to see if you recognise them at all."

"You must be joking! How on earth am I supposed to work out who that person is given the time of night they entered, plus the way they're dressed? Frankly, I think you're being grossly unfair to put me in such a position."

"Admittedly, it was a long shot. Don't worry. I'm sure it'll come to light sooner or later. Another reason we're here is to speak to Belinda Moss."

"Of course. May I ask why you need to speak to her? Because she was the one who found Jess if I recall rightly?"

"Partially, and also because we have it on good authority that Jess and Belinda had a brief confrontation a few weeks ago. Are you telling me that you're unaware of any issues they had between them?"

"This is the first I've heard about it."

"Dave, can you go and find Belinda? Ask her to come in for a chat while I bring Susan up to speed."

Dave nodded and left the office. As soon as the door was closed, Kayli filled Susan in on what Jess's sister had told her.

Susan was clearly mortified by the news and collapsed into her chair. "Bloody hell! I didn't have a clue. I'll be having words with her when you're gone. No one—and I mean *no one*—lays a hand on the horses in my care. I'm not surprised Jess was livid. Why didn't she come to me and tell me about the incident?"

"That's a question I fear we're never going to obtain an answer to. It might explain why Belinda was the first to react when Nutmeg came back to the stable alone."

Susan gasped loudly. "Are you suggesting that she killed Jess?"

"Not necessarily. What I'm suggesting is that perhaps guilt played a part in her actions that day."

"Guilt? I don't understand."

"Yes, maybe she felt guilty about hurting Nutmeg, or more to the point, Jess finding out about the incident. Did you pick up on anything between them over the past few weeks?"

"No, absolutely nothing. Most of my time is spent in here, behind that damn desk of mine. I tend to leave most of the day-to-day chores and running of the stables to my capable staff. Maybe I'm guilty of being neglectful in that respect. I abhor anyone who raises a hand to an animal, though, and I'm shocked Belinda would do such a thing."

The reception door opened, then Dave walked in ahead of Belinda.

"Leave this to me," Kayli whispered to Susan. "Hello, Belinda. We won't keep you long."

"What's this about? Have I done something wrong?" Her gaze shifted from Susan to Kayli and Dave. Her hand shook as she brushed back a few hairs from her cheek that had strayed from her ponytail.

"We just wanted a little chat about your take on what happened the day of the accident. That's all. There's nothing to be worried about. Here, take a seat." Kayli pulled out a chair from the reception desk.

Belinda, still looking as if she might be in shock, sat in the chair and glanced up at Kayli, who had perched on the edge of the desk.

"Anything I can help you with, you only have to ask. It was a dreadful thing to happen, even more so when it led to Jess's death." A tinge of colour filled Belinda's cheeks.

"Very sad. So, on the day of the accident, you were the first to respond to Nutmeg returning from the woods. Is that right?"

"Yes. It was heartbreaking to see. I knew instantly there was something wrong and rallied the troops immediately. We're thankful that Nutmeg had the sense to return to the stables and didn't run off in the other direction. Otherwise, I don't think we would have found Jess so quickly. It still wasn't enough to save her, though, was it?" Her gaze drifted down to the floor in front of her.

"Sadly not. How did you and Jess get on?"

Belinda's head snapped up. "Fine. The same as all the other owners who stable their horses here."

"Is that right?" Kayli asked, her smile never slipping. "Only we've heard to the contrary."

Again, Belinda's startled gaze drifted over the three of them. She shifted uncomfortably in her chair, crossed her feet at the ankles, and slipped her hands between her thighs.

Kayli suspected that was to prevent them from shaking. "I'm not sure what you're talking about. Care to enlighten me?"

"Word has it that you and Jess fell out with each other a few weeks prior to Jess's death. Can you tell us what happened?"

Her gaze dropped again for an instant when she glanced up at Kayli again her eyes were filled with bulging tears. "It was a terrible mistake and one that I regret every night when I go over the events of that day."

"Stop wittering and get on with it, woman," Susan snapped. She folded her arms across her chest and tapped her foot impatiently.

"I didn't think it was much at the time, but upon reflection, I assure you I'm totally ashamed of what I did."

"Ha, because you got caught, you mean!" Susan bit back sharply.

"Please, Susan, let Belinda tell us in her own words." Kayli jumped in quickly. "Go on, Belinda."

"Jess found out that I had struck her horse a few days ago. Someone around here must have snitched on me."

"Good, I'm glad I employ at least some people with an ounce of decency in them. You disgust me."

Belinda's mouth dropped open for a little while, Kayli suspected that gave her time to think of what to say next. "I'm truly sorry. I've never laid a hand on a horse before this occurred or since. I swear I haven't. He frustrated me. Refused to do as he was told, and I lashed out. The thing is, I forgot I had my keys in my hand when I struck him. This caused a graze on his neck, and when Jess came in that day, she saw the graze and came after me. Which, of course, she had every right to do. I pleaded with her not to tell Susan, fearing that I would lose my job. She agreed if I swore that I'd never lay another angry hand on a horse again. Believe me when I say that was an easy thing to agree to. I hated myself for what I did to Nutmeg. It haunts me to this very day, and I can't see that dissipating either."

"You disgust me. If I'd heard about this sooner, I would have given you your damn marching orders. How dare you attack any animal, let alone a beautiful stallion like Nutmeg! Once the inspector has finished speaking to you, I want you to pack up your stuff and leave my premises. You no longer have a job here, and there's no point you putting me down for a reference either. I'll ensure all the stables in the area avoid you like the plague. No one—do you hear me?—*no one* strikes an animal in my care. I will not tolerate any form of animal abuse."

"That's not fair, Susan. It was a one-off that I regret ever happening. Jess had forgiven me for my misdemeanour. Why can't you?"

Kayli was willing to take a back seat and let Susan tear into her staff member, hoping that Belinda would let something of interest slip.

Susan scoffed. "Why should I?" Her eyes narrowed. "Did you break in here?"

Belinda's hand drifted into her hair, and she scratched the side of her head. "What is that supposed to mean? Why the dickens would I break in here when I work here?" She looked at Kayli to get clarification on the comment.

But it was Susan who answered her with a vehement tongue. "Because someone broke in here, and yes, we have the evidence to back up such a claim. They sabotaged Jess's saddle, which, in turn, led to her death."

Belinda shot out of her chair and flew at Susan. Dave managed to grab Belinda's raised fist before it connected with Susan's face.

"That'll do. Back off, lady," he ordered, steering her back to her chair. "Sit down."

"She can't say that to me. Where is this coming from? I've admitted my guilt to hurting Nutmeg. I swear I didn't do the things she said. I *swear*." Tears dripped onto her cheeks.

Something about the woman's reaction told Kayli that she was being honest. "We have clear evidence that someone broke into the premises. The CCTV footage shows this person going into Nutmeg's stall and emerging a few minutes later."

"Well, it wasn't *me*. How the hell did they get in? Did someone forget to lock the gate?" Belinda asked, glaring at Susan.

Kayli shook her head. "No, the person climbed over the gate. Look, we're not suggesting that you're responsible for this, but do you have any idea who would do it? Did Jess fall out with someone else around here who we don't know about?"

"No... I don't know. What I'm trying to say is that I don't know. I'm not into idle gossip."

"No, you just go down the animal-abuse route instead," Susan said snidely.

"Okay, Susan, you've made your feelings perfectly clear on the subject. We need to get past that incident and concentrate on who could be responsible for Jess's death. My take is that Belinda is not the person in the video."

Susan stared at Kayli. "What? You're kidding me? How the hell can you say that after her track record? As far as I know, no one else around here has fallen out with Jess."

"Two points I'd like to raise about your statement. The first is you didn't have a clue that the incident between Belinda and Jess had occurred until we told you, so how do you know that another member of your staff hasn't fallen out with Jess in the past? And second, thinking about things logically, why would Belinda go to the trouble of breaking in when she has access to the stables and all the equipment during her working day?"

Susan's shoulders slumped. "You're right. Maybe I'm guilty of overreacting after what I learnt this morning."

"Apology accepted," Belinda mumbled.

"Don't effing push it, lady. As soon as the inspector leaves, I'll work out how much I owe you in wages and you're out of here."

Belinda shrugged. "Whatever. Like you've never made a mistake in your damn life."

"I've never struck a defenceless animal, I know that much. You make me sick."

"All right, ladies. Less of the aggression. It's not getting us anywhere. Belinda, do you recall hearing another member of staff discussing any possible fallouts they'd had with Jess?"

"Ha! I wouldn't put it past her to make something up now," Susan said.

Belinda shook her head and chewed on her lip. "As if I would. No, I can't think of anything. Surely, if this was down to anyone working at the stables, they would sneak in there and do the damage that you're referring to during their shift. None of this makes sense. Jess was such a nice lady. Crikey, if she wasn't, then Susan would have heard about what I did to Nutmeg long ago."

"I think you're right," Kayli replied. "Well, the footage from the CCTV cameras clearly shows this person knew their way around the stables."

Standing behind Belinda, Dave nodded his agreement.

"So what next?" Susan asked. "Do you need to speak to the rest of the staff?"

"Would you have any objections to that?"

"Not in the slightest. Have you finished with her?" Susan asked, rudely pointing at Belinda. She was definitely showing a different side of her nature.

"I think we've finished with Belinda now." She took a card from her pocket and gave it to Belinda. "If you think of anything that might prove useful to our investigation, will you ring me?"

"Of course I will. Susan, is there any way you'll reconsider your decision? You know how much I love working here and how much I need this job."

"You should have thought about that before you struck Nutmeg. When I employed you, I made it clear from day one what the consequences would be to anyone who ill-treats an animal at these stables. You shouldn't be surprised by my decision in the slightest, and I'm standing firm on this one. If I let it slip, the rest of the staff will see me as a walkover. Pack up your belongings and come back here to collect what's owed to you before you leave."

Belinda's eyes rolled up to the ceiling. "God help you if ever you make a single mistake in your life. That's all it was. A simple mistake that has cost me *everything*."

"You should have thought about that before, shouldn't you? Stop trying to guilt-trip me. It won't wash."

Defeated, Belinda stood and walked towards the door. "I'm sorry it has come to this. I liked Jess a lot. I hope you find her killer soon."

"Thanks, Belinda. Good luck finding another job."

"She's gonna need that," Susan said bitterly.

Once the door closed, Kayli looked at Susan. "If you don't mind me saying, I think you've overreacted by sacking her for one slight mistake."

"I do mind you saying, Inspector. I have a reputation to uphold. If word got out that the staff beat the horses, my business would go up in smoke within a few days. Call my actions self-preservation if you will. I refuse to feel guilty. She was in the wrong and was punished accordingly for her stupid actions. Now, back to business. Do you want to question the rest of the staff?"

"We'll agree to differ on that one, but I understand your reasoning. Do you have many?"

"There are three on duty today. Would you like to question them in here? I can make myself scarce for a few hours if you like."

"That would be brilliant. Thank you, Susan."

She left the office.

"Ouch! She's sure got a temper on her," Dave said the instant the door closed behind her.

"Yep. I wasn't expecting that. If it's like she said about self-preservation, then I suppose I can understand her reaction. I can't help feeling sorry for Belinda, all the same."

"Yeah, I'm inclined to think along those lines, too."

Kayli gestured towards the door. "Here's the first interviewee now."

~ ~ ~

The interviews only took an hour, and nothing new came from any of the three women. What did come across was how much Jess was liked around the stables. All the women were still upset about her passing and devastated to hear that she had been murdered. One of the women saw fit to hint at Belinda possibly doing the deed but rescinded her accusation when Kayli told her that she had just been sacked.

Dave went in search of Susan to tell her that she could have her office back.

When Susan walked in, her eyes were red as if she'd been crying.

"Is everything all right?" Kayli asked, tilting her head in concern.

"Yes, just me being silly. I've never had to sack a member of staff in that way before. I suppose I'm feeling a little guilty now that I've had time to reflect on my behaviour."

"Does that mean you're reconsidering giving Belinda her job back?"

"Certainly not," Susan snapped. "Please don't misinterpret what I said as me thinking I was in the wrong. I most certainly wasn't. I have standards I need to uphold. My staff are aware of those standards when they're first employed. It's in their contract. If she believes I've treated her unfairly, she can take me to court and let a judge decide who is right or wrong."

"I understand. I honestly believe in her case it was a one-off. Maybe when the dust has settled, you'll think about that and even reconsider taking her back. She seemed a nice enough person to me."

"I doubt it. Do you need anything else from me, or can I get back to work now?"

Kayli sighed. Her persuasion techniques were way off the mark with Susan. "We're done. Although we might come back a second time to question your staff if any other evidence comes our way."

"Very well." Susan returned to her desk and opened a file, putting an end to the conversation.

Kayli and Dave left the office and made their way back to the car.

"A bit harsh, wasn't it?" Dave said. "Her sacking the woman like that."

"Yes and no. I can see Susan's point of view but I'm not sure I would have the courage to end someone's career and condemn any further chances they have of continuing in a career they love."

"She was pretty annoyed when you pointed that out to her."

"Maybe Susan is the type of person who hates others showing up her failings. Never mind, let's not dwell on matters that don't concern us."

"True. We're no further forward to finding out who the culprit is, though, unless…"

Kayli pressed the button on her key fob to open the door and looked over the roof at him. "Unless?"

"Unless Susan recognised the person, and that's why she turned out to be so bristly with us."

Kayli shook her head. "I doubt it. But I'm willing to keep that theory in mind."

"Where are we going now?"

"I think a trip to the ex-wife should be next on the agenda, don't you?"

"I'm sure it will be an interesting visit."

CHAPTER EIGHT

Cordelia Porter's address was in a small village on the outskirts of Bristol called Barrow Gurney. After driving around the narrow country lanes for almost three quarters of an hour, looking for the house, Kayli gave in and stopped at the post office in the village to ask for the directions.

The woman behind the counter drew Kayli a helpful map, which led to the cottage within minutes. Kayli couldn't help comparing the quaint thatched house to the house Jess had called home. It was a stark contrast between modern and traditional. Some might even have described the cottage as having an old-world charm. Kayli knew which design she preferred. Traditional charm meant only one thing in her mind: spiders. She shuddered at the thought of the creatures and their cobwebs.

"Do these types of places give you the willies, too?" Dave asked as they wove their way up the curved path, through a fabulous display of cottage garden plants, to the front door.

"Not sure it gives me the willies, as you put it. I can't abide the thought of spiders dropping on my head from all the authentic beams we're about to encounter."

"Let's hope she's renovated the place and torn it to bits inside."

Kayli sniggered. "The thought of someone bothering to buy a place of this age to wreck it like that…well, it just doesn't bear thinking about. This place must have cost a small fortune to buy."

"You're not wrong. I reckon seven to eight hundred thousand easily."

Kayli rang the ornate bell beside the front door.

Not long after, the door was opened by a smartly dressed lady, peering over a pair of glasses perched on the end of her nose, she asked, "Can I help you?"

"Are you Cordelia Porter?"

Her brow furrowed, and she removed her glasses. "I am. Who wants to know?"

Kayli and Dave flashed their warrant cards. "DI Kayli Bright and DS Dave Chaplin from the Avon and Somerset Constabulary. Do you mind if we come in for a chat, Mrs. Porter?"

"Not until you tell me what this is all about."

"We have a few questions to ask you about your ex-husband."

Her frown deepened. "What about him? He's an ex for a reason. If he's in some kind of trouble, then that has nothing to do with me. You're aware that he's remarried, aren't you?"

"I am. Please, it would be better if we spoke inside."

The woman grunted and threw back the front door. It slammed against the wall. Kayli and Dave followed the woman. The hallway was the only part of the house that was free from any beams. Someone had renovated it entirely but had kept the large beams as features. They had been painstakingly sandblasted and were now far lighter in colour than any beam Kayli had seen in a place similar to this before.

"You have a beautiful home. Have you lived here long?" she asked, trying to get back on the woman's good side once more after the anger she'd expressed towards them at the front door.

"Thank you. My ex and I bought it years ago. Over the last five years, I have renovated it room by room. I still have a few of the bedrooms left to do. It's exhausting work. Of course, this place is Grade II listed, which makes the renovation work so much harder. The listed building consent needs to be adhered to one hundred percent, or they come down heavy on you. Without the proper approval, nothing is allowed to be altered. It's very frustrating at times."

"I can imagine. Looks like it was worth all the effort, though. You must be thrilled with the result."

"I am, although very tired after going through the traumatic work. We're still finding dust in places we didn't know existed, months after finishing the renovations."

"I bet."

"Do you want to come through to the kitchen? How about a nice pot of tea? Sorry for my foul mood. I hate to be disrupted when I'm doing needlepoint."

"You don't have to apologise. A coffee would be nice, if it's not too much trouble."

"Come through. I'll stick the kettle on. I made some biscuits this morning. Would you like one?"

"We'd love one, thanks," Dave was quick to answer.

"Take a seat in the garden room. I won't be long." She pointed to a conservatory off the back of the kitchen that was circular in shape and built from oak and glass.

The beautiful room took Kayli's breath away. Quality soft furnishings adorned the chairs and the tiled floor, picking up the vibrant colours in the garden just beyond the windows. "This is fabulous if you don't mind me saying. My mother and father would absolutely love one of these on the back of their house."

"I'm glad you like it. I have to say I tend to spend most of my time in that room, in the summer anyway. Although I have installed underfloor heating, I still don't use it much in the winter because the outlook isn't so pretty, I suppose. It's so hard choosing plants that give the garden life in the winter months. When people see colour in the garden, it gives them a kind of peace and tranquillity. Wouldn't you agree? Or is that simply me being foolish?"

"I can totally see where you're coming from. I'm not a gardening expert in the slightest. Maybe they'll come up with some flowing shrubs that will adapt to our changing climate."

"I hope you're right. One year is totally different to the next once September has passed. Here you go. Help yourselves." She placed a tray on the small table between the two sofas.

Dave was the first to reach for one of the chocolate cookies on the plate.

Kayli handed him a side plate to catch the crumbs and helped herself to one of the biscuits, which melted in her mouth in an instant. "These are delicious. Is it a family recipe?"

"I suppose you could say that. I used to make them with my grandmother when I was a child. I hope the coffee isn't too strong. Sorry it's instant. I find it hard to judge the right amount of granules to put in, being a tea drinker."

"No need for you to worry. It's just right. Thank you."

"Now that's out of the way, perhaps you'd care to enlighten me as to why you're here?"

Kayli wiped the crumbs off her top lip and withdrew her notebook from her pocket. "Have you been in contact with your ex-husband recently?"

The woman's eyes dropped to the cup and saucer while she stirred her cup of tea. "Depends what you mean by recently."

"In the last month or so."

"Off and on. We try to avoid each other wherever possible. As I've already stated, we're exes for a reason, Inspector."

"I understand. May I ask what the contact was regarding, if you don't tend to get along?"

"Our son. As much as I'd love Wesley to be exempt from the decisions forced upon us by our son's future, he would have my guts for garters and drag me through the courts to ensure he had his say."

"I see. Does your son get on with his father?"

"He tolerates him. Life is far happier for Patrick without his father's interference, if I can put it that way."

"You can." Kayli sighed. "Are you aware of what has gone on in your ex-husband's life in the past few days?"

"I am, painfully aware. I've reached out to Wes to offer my condolences, but that's as far as my sympathy gene will allow me to go, I'm afraid. If that sounds harsh, then so be it. That man put me through the mire during our marriage and since our divorce was finalised."

"Sorry to hear that. May I ask in what respect?"

Cordelia inhaled a large breath then sipped at her drink. "I'd rather not go into details, if you don't mind. I'd prefer not drag up the past that I have locked away in a dark corner of my mind."

"Okay, maybe you'll reconsider as our conversation progresses. Can you tell me if you got on with Jessica Porter?"

"I can't say I really knew her that well. She seemed a nice enough person on the odd occasion I've seen her, but I can't say any more than that."

"How did your son get on with her?"

"He accepted her for his father's sake. You know what boys are like."

"I do. A law unto themselves at times, with their hormones raging at that age, right?"

Cordelia smiled. "You've nailed it. I feel sorry she's no longer with us. I hope Wes doesn't start coming around here, bothering me."

"Bothering you? Do you think that's likely?"

"Oh, I don't know. It may have been a throwaway suggestion on my part. They've had the odd spat over the years, and Wes has shown up on my doorstep, looking for a place to stay until they patched things up."

"Was Jess aware of this?"

"I'm not sure. I couldn't see him on the street. He's my son's father, after all. I always emphasised that the situation was a temporary one from the moment he stepped foot in the house. He seemed grateful to have somewhere to stay and always went back to her within a few days anyway. So no big deal."

"Did this happen regularly?"

"Not really. I suppose only a few times over the years since they've been married. Hardly what I'd call a regular occurrence."

"Can you give me an idea how many times?"

"Casting my mind back—because I'd rather not dwell on it—I suppose two, possibly three or four times."

Kayli nodded. "For a matter of days or longer?"

"Definitely days. Let's just say that I didn't make life easy for him when he was here. I told him he had to earn his keep. That was totally alien to Wes when I lived with him. As far as I can tell, he's altered slightly now, at least he had before Jess died."

"So their relationship was volatile at times?"

Cordelia glanced past Kayli and out the window to the garden beyond. "I think that would be too strong a term to use. Maybe not always content at times. I was keen to keep out of it. As long as Wes paid his maintenance for Patrick every month on time, then I was a happy bunny."

"Were there any instances when he neglected to pay?"

"Once or twice. I threatened to drag him through the family court, and he appeared to buck his ideas up after that. You really shouldn't have to do that if your son is entitled to that money, right?"

"I agree. These men should take on the responsibility of financially supporting the kids they're keen to spawn. Far too many men walk away from their families these days."

"Exactly. I was determined that wouldn't happen with us, especially as he pleaded with me to start a family before I was truly ready. I had a fantastic job in London as a stock broker until I met him. He persuaded me to give it all up and move to Bristol to be with him."

"Glancing around, I can see you seem to have come out of the marriage with a lovely home."

"Looks are deceiving. It's mortgaged to the hilt. I love it here, though. I was prepared to go the whole hog with the renovations so that I could stay here without imagining him in the rooms. Do you know what I mean?"

"I can understand that. Do you work now, Cordelia?"

"I do. I work from home, selling stocks and shares on a part-time basis. I make enough money to meet the mortgage and to cover all the bills. Once Patrick is at uni, I'm going to increase my hours at work."

"Is Wes going to help you finance Patrick's education?"

"He says he is. That's why I've been in touch with him lately, through necessity rather than desire."

"Won't that be a struggle for him? Having two kids close to the same age? Won't Cathy be going off to uni soon?"

"She has a few years at college ahead of her yet. Anyway, that's not my problem. He'll have to get off his backside and work longer hours or get his skivvies to."

"At the car-cleaning business? Do you know how that is doing?"

"Haven't got a clue. It's really none of my concern as I'm no longer married to the man."

"Can I ask why you separated?"

She rolled her eyes. "In a nutshell, because of his damn wandering eye. I think most men are the bloody same. The ones I've had the misfortune to date anyway. They seem to puff out their chests even if you show a teeny bit of interest in them. Think they're desirable beyond words. Christ! I sound really bitter but I'm not. I promise you. Put it this way: if another man never came into my life, I wouldn't have any regrets."

Kayli smiled and nodded. "Okay, going back to why Wes and Jess fell out on the odd occasion—can you give me an idea about that?"

"It was mostly about money, I think. Okay, I'd rather not get involved in this if you don't mind. It's really got nothing to do with me."

"Sorry, but I have to push you a little bit further. If their arguments were regarding money, surely in a roundabout way, that would concern you because of Patrick."

"Okay, you win. But I'd rather stay out of it all the same."

"Are you implying that you do know and that you'd rather not divulge why?"

Her gaze met Kayli's, and she nodded. "Please, I don't want any trouble coming to my door. I live a peaceful life with my son and I'd much rather keep it that way."

"What if I promise to keep your name out of things?"

"You think that's likely to happen if this ends up in court?"

"I'll do my very best. Please, Cordelia, if there's a dark secret waiting to be discovered, then I think we should know about it."

She buried her head in her hands for a few moments.

Kayli eyed Dave with concern.

Finally, Cordelia dropped her hands into her lap and exhaled a large sigh. "He has a gambling problem. But you haven't heard that from me. As soon as I heard about that, I took over the deeds to this house. It put a strain on our marriage from the day I found out. I was glad when he admitted to having an affair with someone at work, because it gave me an excuse to kick him out of the family home. I'm very cautious with money, and it rankled me to think it slipped through his fingers so quickly. I loved him deeply but I wasn't prepared to put myself through that crap any longer."

"Has he visited his son much over the years? I mean, been there for him without you having to prod him into action to make an effort to see Patrick?"

"Hit and miss on that front. Patrick accepted that he would always come second to Cathy in his father's eyes."

"That's so sad for your son."

"He's not alone. There are plenty of children in his class who are in the same situation. Families never appear to stay together for the sake of the children any longer. It used to be an unusual situation for a child to come from a broken home back in the day. Now it seems to be becoming the norm."

"I fear you're right. Does Patrick have any form of relationship with his father?"

"Not really. He's a good enough kid and applies himself well at school. He's just been awarded a place at Cambridge University. We're thrilled about that."

"We? Are you including Wesley in that 'we'?"

"Yes, although initially, I meant that Patrick and I are both thrilled. Once Patrick shared the news with his father, all Wes was concerned about was how much it was going to cost to put Patrick through university. He came here a few weeks ago, creating merry hell, and Patrick ended up shouting at him. Ordered him to leave because he was upsetting me."

"And what was Wes's reaction to that?" Kayli asked, her interest soaring.

"He shrugged and walked out. Never tried to reason with his son. Just accepted that Patrick was angry. What type of father allows that to happen?" she asked Kayli bitterly as she wiped away a stray tear.

"Please, don't upset yourself. Some divorces never seem clear-cut and more often than not are full of angst. Your son is a credit to you because of the way you've brought him up. With his father being so distant, you must have a very close bond with Patrick."

She smiled. "I do. He's an exceptional kid. Of course he has his moments. What teenager doesn't? In his father's eyes, he's a rebel."

"A rebel? Care to elaborate why his father should perceive him as such?"

"He got in with a bad crowd. They stole a car and torched it. He was arrested for still being at the scene when the police showed up. The others had scarpered, but he was found trying to pour water on the vehicle. He'd bought some bottled water from the shop up the road and was squirting it on the car, silly lad. The thought was there, though."

"Are you telling us that he was a bystander when the incident occurred in the first place?"

"No, he admitted that he was involved, but when he realised the others had the intention of setting the car alight, he tried to prevent it. They called him a wuss and took off without him. You'd think the system would have gone lightly on him, but it didn't. He even gave up the names of the other boys, hoping for a lighter sentence."

"Did he get one?"

"Yes and no. He now only has to do two hundred hours community service. It's nothing to the rest of the gang, who were sent down for their part. But he still has to live with the stigma of being a grass and has to watch his back in case the gang find some way of exacting their revenge."

"He's a brave lad. Not every teenage boy would have the balls to speak out the way he has. You must be proud of him."

"I am. He regrets his actions more than anything now. The last time his father saw him, they had words. Wes tends to shout first before he's had time to assess the situation properly. Patrick ended up walking out on his father mid-argument."

"I bet Wes isn't the type of man who appreciates people, especially his son, walking away from him."

"You're right. Between you and me, Patrick confided in me that if he never saw his father again, it would be a relief for him. That upset me, to see the vehement way he told me that and the hurt I witnessed in his eyes."

"Maybe it would be better if Patrick didn't see his father in the future if that's what he wants."

She gasped. "I would never suggest such a thing. I'll support my son in his decision-making but I still think he should see his father. I'd rather not determine his actions for him either way. The choice has to be his. Wes can be such a prick at times, you'll have to take my word on that one."

Kayli nodded. "Okay, if there's nothing else, then I think we should make a move."

"I can't think of anything. I hope you find whoever is responsible for Jess's death soon."

Dave and Kayli followed Cordelia back through the house to the front door, where they discovered it had started to rain.

"Thank you for the drink and the chat, Cordelia. You've been most helpful."

"You're welcome." She closed the door gently behind them as they ran for cover to the car.

"Hmm…well, that was certainly interesting," Dave said, sweeping the wet hair back from his forehead.

"Wasn't it just? I think the first thing we should do is find out for ourselves if the incident with the car panned out the way it did, or if we've just heard the biased version from a distraught parent."

Dave turned to face her. "You're doubting her version of the events?"

"I don't know what to think at present or who I can trust just yet. I'm picking up bad vibes about this family, and at the moment, I can't figure out who is telling the truth and who is covering their backs by telling more lies. Let's go with the facts at our disposal and work back from there."

"Cordelia came across as pretty level-headed to me. You have to admire the way she's brought up her son by herself."

"Oh, I do. There's no doubt in my mind she's done an admirable job of that, but there's still a niggling doubt gnawing at my insides. Interesting that she should mention that Wes has a gambling problem.

We need to find out more about that side of things, whether it's more than that, like an addiction, perhaps."

"We should get Donna on it when we get back to the station. What now? We still have to visit Jess's parents, don't forget."

Kayli sighed. "I hadn't forgotten. I was hoping to visit them when I had more information to go on. I'm sure they'll be demanding answers that we simply can't supply right now. I'm inclined to leave it for a day or two."

Dave frowned. "That's unusual for you, but I have to agree."

"Glad about that. Let's return to base and bounce some ideas around with the others."

~ ~ ~

As soon as she and Dave returned to the station, Kayli gave Donna a brief rundown of her conversation with Cordelia Porter. She then asked Graeme to track down the details of the incident involving Patrick Porter. Afterwards, she grabbed a coffee and drifted into her office to tackle the post for the next half an hour or so.

Distracted by the case, she opened one brown envelope then set the contents aside to write down a few things that were bugging her. The case was proving to be rather more complex than she had anticipated it would be.

They still had to return to see Wes, and she wasn't happy with the way their last meeting had ended. They also had to slot in a visit to Jess's parents. Plus, the ex-boyfriends would need to be traced and contacted, as well. Kayli doodled on the top of the page before she added another name to the list of people she needed to speak with: Deanne Mitchell, Jess's ex-best friend. They were drowning in possible suspects, and she had the feeling her team would be stretched over the next few days.

Leaving the remainder of the post unopened, she returned to the outer office to discuss the situation with her team. Once she entered the room, Kayli looked over to Donna, who had her head down, busily making notes. Kayli crossed the room briskly. "Everything all right, Donna?"

"Not sure, boss. I think I've uncovered something that needs your immediate attention. Let me finish jotting these notes down, and I'll be with you."

Kayli stood behind the sergeant's chair and peered over her shoulder at the notes she was scribbling and let out a long whistle. "Holy crap! How could we have missed this before?"

Donna turned to face her. "Sorry, boss. I should have delved into the financial side of things from the get-go."

Kayli squeezed Donna's shoulder. "Nonsense, you've had enough to do with the tasks I've already set you. Bloody hell. I dread to think where this information is going to lead us. Well done, Donna. You're the best."

CHAPTER NINE

The team gathered around, and Donna filled everyone in on what she'd discovered about Wesley Porter's gambling addiction.

"I pulled up both Wes's and Jess's bank accounts, and bingo! I found several large deposits showing up in Wes's account that had been transferred from Jess's."

"Was she bailing him out? His business perhaps?" Dave queried.

"I'm more inclined to go down the gambling route, given what Cordelia told us, although you have raised a good point. We need to get onto Companies House, see how the business is stacking up financially."

"Do you want me to ring around the local casinos, see if he's got a tab of sorts?"

"I think we should. Christ, the way things are looking, Jess handed over three hundred grand to him. That's hardly a drop in the ocean."

"We could always ask him about it," Dave suggested.

"I'd rather not do that until we have something concrete to back up our claims, Dave. Let's spend the rest of the day going over the financial side of things and go from there. Maybe I should drop by and have a chat with Jess's folks after all."

"Want me to go with you?" Dave asked, rising to his feet.

"No. I'd rather go alone. You oversee things here. I need you to dig, dig, dig, and don't stop until you've uncovered every penny that man has spent in the last six months."

"That's going to take us bloody ages," Dave grumbled.

"It has to be done, partner. I'm also wondering whether to put a surveillance team on him." Just then Kayli's mobile rang. "Caroline? How can I help?"

"Hi, I wanted to bring you up to speed on what's going on at my end," the pathologist said. "I've now released Jessica Porter's body to the funeral home. Apparently, the husband was making a bit of a nuisance of himself with my boss, demanding to know when she could be buried."

"Very interesting. Did he say why the rush?" Kayli asked, raising an eyebrow in Dave's direction.

"Nope, only that he and the family were keen to get her funeral out of the way."

"He was speaking on behalf of all the family or just him and Cathy?"

"I can't answer that, sorry. Does it make a difference?"

"Not really. I'm heading out to visit Jess's parents now so I'll see for myself."

"Good. Are you any further forward with the case?"

"Yes and no. We think we've unearthed a possible motive but we'd like to uncover more proof before we pounce on that. I have to run. I'll ring you when we have more, Caroline."

"You bloody tease. Give me a clue…are you leaning towards the husband being the killer?"

Kayli laughed. "You're terrible. Yes, I think so. I'll be in touch soon." She jabbed her finger at the button to end the call. "Right, I'm going before I get interrupted again. You got the gist of that call, I take it, Dave?"

"Porter has been badgering for his wife's body to be released?"

"He has. I think it's strange that he seems to be in a panic to get her buried—or cremated. Not sure which."

"I have my suspicions about that."

Kayli crossed her arms and tapped her foot impatiently. "Are you going to keep me dangling for long, partner?"

"Life insurance!"

Kayli's eyes widened as her brain kicked up a gear. "Damn, the most obvious reason of all. Look into that for me while I'm out. I need to go now."

"Leave it with me. Give me a ring if you need help."

She smiled reassuringly. "I'll be fine. Stick with it, guys. I'm seeing a glimmer at the end of a very long tunnel now."

~ ~ ~

Pulling into the quiet crescent, she leaned over the steering wheel in search of the house numbers. Finally, she located the number she was after and pulled up outside the large bungalow that was set back off the road behind an immaculately kept front garden that consisted of dozens of topiary hedges sculpted into animals. Kayli couldn't help but be impressed by the display that greeted her as she approached the front door. She rang the bell, and a grey-haired woman appeared at the bay window. Kayli waved at the woman, who disappeared and reappeared instantly at the front door as it opened.

"Hello, Mrs. Watson. I'm DI Kayli Bright. I'm the investigating officer working on your daughter's case."

"Oh, I see. Do you have some news for me? Amelia told us that you believe my daughter was murdered. I find that hard to believe."

"Would it be okay if I stepped in for a few minutes?"

"Of course. I'll just call my husband. He's pottering around in the back garden, trying to keep his mind occupied."

"Is he the topiary expert?" Kayli pointed at the beautiful sculptured hedges dominating the front garden.

"He is," Mrs. Watson replied, closing the front door. "He took up the hobby after he retired, because he was getting under my feet. He's become a dab hand at it now, as you can see. We often observe people standing on the pavement, admiring the display. It's nice to have a front garden that is different. Don't you agree? Sorry, I'm prattling on. Come through to the kitchen. Can I get you a tea or coffee?"

"Thank you, a cup of coffee would be wonderful. I agree—your garden certainly draws the eye, even for someone like me who doesn't know the difference between a spade and a fork."

"You'd soon learn the difference after ten minutes talking to my gardening expert. Let me give him a shout, and then I'll make a drink. Please, take a seat."

Kayli warmed to the woman immediately. The kitchen was reminiscent of her grandmother's country kitchen that she used to enjoy visiting as a child. She always felt safe at her grandmother's house. It always had a calming effect over her for some reason.

"Gerald, dear. There's a nice policewoman to see us. I think she's the same woman Amelia told us about. Do you want to come in and listen to what she has to say?"

"I'll be right with you, love. Of course I want to hear what she has to say."

Mrs. Watson closed the back door then filled the kettle. She prepared a tray with china cups and saucers before she addressed Kayli again. "He won't be long now. He prefers to wash his hands in the utility room rather than dirty the kitchen sink, unlike other men."

"There's no rush. Have you lived here long, Mrs. Watson?"

"Please, call me Mary. Gosh, the years go by so quickly as you get older. I suppose we've been here about fifteen years now, give or take a year or two. We downsized from a two-storey detached house to the bungalow well before we had to. I think the move was a wise one. We're both in excellent health. Not sure we would have been if we'd kept the old rambling house. This house is so much easier to keep clean."

The back door opened, and in stepped a grey-haired gentleman with a ruddy complexion. He smiled at Kayli as he slipped off his gardening shoes. "Hello there. Tell me, what news do you have of our daughter's murder?"

"At least take a seat before you start bombarding the inspector with your questions, Gerald," Mary chastised with a tut and a smile.

"Hello, Mr. Watson. Pleased to meet you. I've been admiring your expertise in the front garden." She smiled warmly as the man pulled out the chair opposite her.

"Thank you. It keeps me out of trouble."

Mary placed the drinks in front of each of them then sat in the chair next to her husband. She looked worried in spite of the slight smile on her face. "Do you have any news for us yet or is it too soon for that?"

"Things are always a little slow at the beginning of an investigation of this nature. I'm sorry for your loss. I thought it would be better not to show up on your doorstep for a few days, give you a chance to grieve properly."

"We're done with the grieving. Now we're angry and want answers. Who would do such a dreadful thing to our daughter?" Gerald asked. He reached for his wife's hand.

"Gerald's right. We're desperate for answers. Do you have an idea who would do this to our beautiful daughter? She's never hurt anyone in her life. We can't imagine anyone being so angry with her that they would intentionally set out to take her life."

"I don't have a definitive answer for you at present. My team are working extremely hard on the case. I want to assure you of that.

Maybe you'll allow me to ask you some questions that will help the investigation gather momentum?"

"Fire away," Mary said.

Kayli withdrew her notebook and flipped open to a blank page. "Maybe we can start by discussing what state your daughter's marriage was in?"

"Good, as far as we know," Gerald replied.

"Yes, I'd go along with that," Mary said. "Why?"

"I went to see Wesley the other day but received a brusque reception. Unfortunately, Cathy happened to walk in behind me just as I was telling Wes we believe Jess's death is suspicious. He was livid and asked my partner and I to leave before we had a proper chance to raise any questions."

"Oh dear, that was unfortunate. And you think we can fill you in?"

"I was hoping that, yes. Were they happy, Wes and Jess?"

Mary nodded. "I think so. That's always the impression I had. Are you suggesting that they weren't?"

"Not really." Kayli exhaled a breath. The Watsons were a nice couple, and she was conscious they were still grieving in spite of their reassurances to the contrary. She didn't want to cause them any unnecessary upset, the way she had Cathy. "During the investigation, something has come to our attention that we're delving into further."

"And that is?" Gerald asked.

Kayli hesitated for a brief moment before she answered, "Large sums of money were transferred from Jess's bank account in the last few months."

Jess's parents stared at each other in shock before Gerald looked back at Kayli. "You've followed the route of that money, I take it?"

Kayli nodded. "We have. It wasn't difficult. The money went into Wes's personal account."

"What? Have you asked him about this?" Gerald demanded.

"Not yet. As I said, this evidence has only just come to our attention. I take it you didn't know about the money?"

"Too right we didn't. I would have tackled them both about it. That money was Jess's inheritance from her grandmother. Her insurance for later life, not to be squandered away. Have you checked Wes's account? Is the money still sitting there?"

"We have, and no, the money has gone. We're doing our best to trace it now. The thing is, we've heard on the grapevine that Wes has, or at least he used to have, a gambling problem."

Gerald banged his clenched fist on the table, rattling the cups and saucers. "Well, no one told us that. Who did you hear this snippet of gossip from? A reliable source, Inspector?"

"His ex-wife, Cordelia Porter."

"What? And you believe her?" Gerald asked, releasing his wife's hand.

"Shouldn't I? Do you know her, Mr. Watson?"

"Of course I know her. I would have no hesitation in calling her a troublemaker. I can't believe you would listen to a word that woman has to say."

"Until we have evidence to hand, we have to listen to and follow up on everything someone is willing to share about people connected to the victim."

"But ex-wives will predictably thrust the knife in—metaphorically speaking, of course—wouldn't they?"

"Normally, I would agree with you. Having spoken to Cordelia myself, I wouldn't say that's the way it came across. If anything, I'd say she was reluctant to tell me about Wes's gambling."

"I can't believe that. She's always been a thorn in Jess's and Wes's sides, demanding more and more money for that wayward lad of hers. As soon as she heard about Jess's inheritance, the demands increased."

"I'm sorry to hear that. As I said, it's simply due diligence to follow up on information we receive. One major point, however, is we have the bank accounts to back up her claims."

"You have evidence of money being transferred. You're aware of our daughter and Wes buying a new dream home, aren't you?"

"I am. According to Amelia, Jess put an extra hundred thousand into the pot to buy the new home, which is beautiful, by the way. But we're talking a substantial amount more than that. About three hundred thousand being transferred, and the rest of the money has gone missing. Can you think of anything else that might have been bought with the extra money?"

"Not off the top of my head. What about you, Mary?"

"No. Our daughter was very frugal with her money. That inheritance meant a lot to her, giving her financial security. The last thing she would do is fritter it away. Maybe the inspector is right, Gerald. My God, if you are, do you think that Wes is guilty of not only taking her money but also killing her?"

Kayli raised her hands in front of her. "Honestly, this is just one avenue we're looking into at present. We have a list of suspects that I still need to speak to. As far as motives go, money is often at the root. Are you telling me that Jess and Wes never argued or fought with each other?"

"No more than other married couples," Mary replied.

Gerald huffed. "All the arguments seem to have concerned that ex-wife and son of his. Maybe Jess handed the money over to keep them quiet for a few months."

"I didn't get that impression when I spoke to Cordelia. She told me that Wes and she had argued recently because he wasn't forthcoming with any money to help fund Patrick going to university."

"Then I'm sorry, because I have no answers," Gerald said. "You mentioned a list of suspects. Do you want to run some names past us, Inspector, see if we can give you any details regarding that person's relationship with our daughter?"

"Okay." She flipped back a few pages and reeled off the names, which included the ex-boyfriends and Deanne Mitchell.

"I know who my money would be on," Gerald said.

"Who?" his wife asked before Kayli got the chance to.

"Carl Longhurst. He was always a shifty bugger to me."

"Do you have any proof to substantiate that claim, Mr. Watson?"

"Nope. You know when you get an inkling about a certain person? I had a dicky tummy every time he used to come round our house to pick Jess up to take her out. I breathed a sigh of relief the day they broke up."

"Did you get the same feeling, Mary?"

Mary shrugged and shook her head. "Can't say I did, no. He always came across as a very charming young man to me."

"One of those men who could charm the knickers off women but who got men's backs up," Gerald admitted.

"That's just you being jealous, Gerald, and you know it."

Kayli laughed inwardly at the slight reprimand Mrs. Watson gave her husband. "Okay, I'll make it a priority for me to seek him out. Apparently, he's recently returned to the country after a long absence away."

Gerald clicked his fingers and pointed at Kayli. "There you go then. What did I tell you? Coincidence? I think not. I'd go round there mob-handed if I were you. Don't trust the little worm one iota."

"I can't agree with my husband, but it might be wise if you spoke to him soon, given that he's only just returned."

"According to Amelia, Jess met up with Carl in town lately for a coffee. Therefore, I'm presuming there were no ill-feelings on Jess's part."

"How strange that Amelia didn't mention it to us," Mary said, looking thoughtful.

"Maybe it slipped her mind. Perhaps there was nothing in it after all, except two old friends meeting up for an innocent chat."

"Ha, I wouldn't bank on that. I'd still question him as if I were a member of the Gestapo," Gerald said.

"I'll question him, you can be assured of that. Is there anyone else you can think of who I should question?"

Mary and Gerald both shook their heads.

Kayli finished the rest of her drink and stood. "I'll leave you to it then and be in touch as soon as I have anything concrete to share with you. Can I ask you to keep this conversation between yourselves until then?"

"Of course," Mary said, standing and moving towards the kitchen door. She walked up the hallway and opened the front door.

Kayli shook her hand. "Thank you for agreeing to speak to me at such a sad time. Oh, by the way, do you know when the funeral will be? I'd like to attend."

"Wes promised he'd ring us as soon as the arrangements had been made."

"You're leaving all the arrangements to him?"

"Yes, I'm not sure I could cope with doing all of that. It's just too raw."

"I understand completely. Sorry for your loss. Here's my card if you should think of anything or ever need to chat about the case."

Mary took the card and nodded. "Thank you. Please do your best to find the person who robbed us of our beautiful daughter, Inspector. We're relying on you."

"You have my word on that. I'll be in touch soon."

Kayli drove away from the house, feeling sorry for the lovely couple she'd just met. She rang the office to see if there was any news. "Dave, it's me. What have you got for me?"

"Nothing much. I've rung a few of the casinos in the area, but they're refusing to dish out that kind of information over the phone."

"Damn. There's only one thing for it then—you're going to have to visit them in person to force their hands."

"Great, thanks for that. I take it I need to go alone."

"Why not? You're not worried, are you? I think you've been watching too many films again. Go on, be brave. I'm on my way to see Carl Longhurst."

"I'd rather tag along with you. How were the parents?"

"Better than I expected. I think it was wise leaving them alone for a few days."

"Why are you going to see the ex? Did they say something about him that has sparked your interest?"

"Sort of. The father said he always had a gut reaction when Carl was around. I'm not sure he had anything to do with Jess's murder or not. I still need to check it out."

"Okay. Touch base once you've seen him."

"I will, my guardian angel. Good luck at the casinos. Go softly. Well, softly at first then give them hell if they refuse to play ball. Threaten them that we'll turn up with a full squad at their busiest time with a warrant in our hands if they refuse to cooperate. That should put the wind up them."

Dave chuckled. "I'll do that, boss. Take care. See you later."

"Be careful."

As she drove to Longhurst's address, Kayli's mind raced with the questions she wanted to ask him. She pulled up outside a small block of flats and parked the car in a space closest to the entrance. She wandered up the stairs, noting how clean the stairwell was compared to some of the other blocks in the Bristol area she'd had the misfortune of visiting lately. She knocked on the door to Longhurst's flat and waited. No answer came, so she knocked a second time. Still no answer. She sighed and tried the next door along the concrete landing.

A young woman with bunches in her hair opened the door. Chewing her gum noisily, she asked, "Yeah, what do you want? I can tell you're the filth."

Kayli issued her a taut smile and produced her warrant card. "I was after your neighbour. Is he around?"

"Does it look like I'm his frigging keeper?" she shouted before slamming the door in Kayli's face.

"Charming. Nice meeting you, too," she grumbled. Kayli walked back down the stairs and jumped in the car. She returned to the station, regretting that she hadn't taken down Dave's itinerary when she'd spoken to him.

~ ~ ~

Dave returned to the station with more interesting news than Kayli had managed to gather in her time on the road. The team assembled around his desk to listen.

"I went to a few of the smaller casinos, thinking he might frequent them more than the larger one in town. I was wrong. I was feeling downbeat by the time I got to Winners Casino."

Kayli raised her hand to stop him. "Any chance you can cut to the point, partner? I'd like to get home to see Mark before he goes to work this evening if at all possible."

Dave tutted and went on with his tale. "Anyway, I was asking around about whether Wesley Porter was a regular visitor when one of the croupiers began to act a little shifty. Her smile dropped when she heard his name, and she avoided eye contact with me from then on."

Kayli folded her arms and nodded. "So what did you find out?"

"Well, she clammed up, so I walked away from her and started asking some of the other croupiers if they knew him. I kept looking back at the girl, and every time I turned her way, I found her staring—or should I say *glaring* at me."

"Yep, sounds dodgy to me, Dave. Did you get a chance to speak to the manager?"

"Eventually, yes. I questioned him about the girl, and she's called Moira. He couldn't really tell me much. But that's where this all gets interesting. I thought I'd have to be heavy-handed with him when I asked about Wes, but he gave up the information willingly."

Kayli motioned with her hand to speed him up.

"I'm getting there. Be patient. Right, here's the good part. Wesley Porter is in debt to the casino to the sum of fifty grand."

Kayli nodded slowly. "Is he now? Well, it took you a long detour around the houses to tell us that fact, but you got there in the end. I think we're all eternally grateful for that."

Dave's eyes narrowed. "That's all the thanks I get for finding out that morsel of information?"

Kayli slapped him on the shoulder. "You're so damn easy to wind up. Good work. It's yet another trail that leads back to the money motive. I'm wondering whether to put Wes under surveillance."

"Why are you deliberating that?" Dave asked.

"I hate doing it to him when he's supposed to be grieving. It simply doesn't sit well with me."

"I could see your point if there wasn't any suspicion attached, but he's our lead suspect now, surely?"

"Okay. We'll start tomorrow, during the day. I doubt he'll be venturing out at night now that he has to take care of Cathy."

"With respect, boss," Donna interjected. "Isn't the daughter sixteen?"

"Point taken. Anyone fancy taking the nightshift in that case?"

Dave's head turned in Graeme's direction.

Graeme shook his head. "Cheers, mate. As it happens, I have a family engagement on tonight. Otherwise, I'd volunteer to do it."

"Great, that only leaves me then," Dave grumbled.

Kayli smiled. "Good man. Let me spend an hour with Mark, and I'll come and join you."

"That's not necessary. You stay at home. I'll do the nightshift, and we'll go from there."

"Under one proviso."

"What's that?"

"You ring me straight away if anything develops."

"Of course I will. Now I'm really hoping something happens just so I can wake you up in the early hours of the morning."

Kayli reached behind her on the desk for a pen and threw it at him. "Okay, let's call it a day and start again tomorrow, with the exception of Dave. Seriously, I really appreciate this, partner. Go home and show up at Wes's house around nine. That'll give you a few hours off."

"Thanks, I'll do that."

"And no sleeping on the job," Graeme added with a grin.

Dave put a hand to his chest. "*Moi?* Would I do that?"

"It has been known in the past when we've been on surveillance together."

Kayli raised an eyebrow. "Oh, it's all coming out now. Well, maybe I'll surprise you during the night in that case, Dave. Ensure you don't take your eye off the ball."

He pulled a face at her. "I'll sit there with Sellotape keeping my eyes open if I have to."

"Glad to hear it. Let's go home, guys."

CHAPTER TEN

Kayli received the call from Dave just as she was getting ready for bed. She cursed under her breath and answered the call. "Hi, Dave. How's it going?"

"I'm on the move. He must have waited to make sure Cathy was asleep and then left the house."

Kayli glanced at the clock on her phone. It was ten after eleven. "Any idea where he's going?"

"I reckon he's en route to the casino. Want me to follow him inside?"

"Yes, but keep your distance. Do you want me to come down and join you?"

"Nah, I'll be fine. Of course I'll give him some space. What do you take me for? Some kind of novice at this game?"

"Sorry, I'm only being overprotective. I'm wide awake anyway, so maybe I should come down there."

"That's entirely up to you. I want to put it on record that I'm not asking you to. That I'm only keeping you informed of what's going on as per your request."

"Noted. Ring me when you get to the location. I'll get dressed in the meantime."

"Talk to you soon."

It was another fifteen minutes before Dave rang her back. Kayli slipped on a pair of jeans and a pullover, ready to leave once he gave her the location. "Where are you?"

"Just pulled up outside Winners Casino. Do you want me to go in after him or wait for you to arrive?"

"I'll be there within ten minutes. Wait for me, and we'll go in together."

"Rightio," Dave said, ending the call.

Kayli raced into the lounge to collect her handbag then rushed out the front door. She pulled up alongside her partner's car a few minutes later.

He smiled and exited his vehicle.

Kayli wound down her window, and he leaned down to speak to her. "Are we going inside?"

"Why not? We're not going to get a feel of what's going on out here."

They marched into the casino. Kayli grudgingly paid the exorbitant entrance fee of fifteen pounds each and entered the vast area. Slot machines lined every wall to the entrance hall. There wasn't a single machine vacant as Kayli and Dave walked past the area into the main part of the casino. Kayli had never been inside one and was in awe of not only the grandeur of the place but also how many punters it held.

"There must be thousands here," she whispered.

"Amazing, right? Does that mean they're all in debt?"

"I wouldn't say that, but who knows?" She shuddered at the thought of people easily losing thousands of pounds on a turn of a card or the frivolous spin of the roulette wheel. She'd never had the urge to bet on the Grand National, let alone sit at a table paying pontoon. She just couldn't see the fascination with spending her hard-earned money in a single night.

Dave nudged her with his elbow. "Suspect at ten o'clock. Hmm…he's chatting with the same girl who was acting suspicious when I visited earlier."

"Interesting. Let's keep an eye on them for a while. They seem very friendly to me—overfriendly, in fact."

"I was thinking the same thing. I wish I could see what his hands are up to. Something more than just doing her job has put that huge smile on her face."

Kayli chuckled. "I find it amusing how your mind works sometimes."

"Hey, if you could've seen the way she was interacting with the punters earlier, you'd soon get where I'm coming from. It's like night and day. Take my word on that."

"Maybe we should split up. He's seen us together. The chances are less likely that he'll identify us if we're at different ends of the room. I'll go left, and you go right."

"Yep, makes sense to me."

They split up and agreed to join up again at the blackjack table, where Wes was sitting alongside the croupier. A large pile of chips sitting in front of him as she got closer to the table.

Are they his winnings? No, it can't be. He's not been here that long. There must be a couple of thousand there at least. How can that be allowed if he's over fifty grand in debt? She shook her head as the realisation set in. *Maybe he's put some kind of collateral up against the debt, like his business or even his house.* She shuddered again at the prospect of all that money seeping through his fingers.

The croupier turned over a couple of cards, one in front of Wes and the other in front of a large man in his fifties who was smoking a huge Cuban cigar. Wes's smile dropped when the Queen of Hearts was placed on his Jack of Clubs and two of diamonds. He threw himself back in his chair and glared at the stout man, who was laughing raucously at him. Anger was evident in Wes's eyes. It was only there for an instant, but she'd spotted it, nonetheless.

He sat forward again and demanded a rematch.

"I love taking money off you, man. I'm up for it. Deal, little lady," the stout man ordered, taking a puff on his cigar.

The croupier seemed unnerved for an instant, until Wes nodded and issued her a special smile. She cut the pack in her own fancy way and distributed two cards to each of the players. They both lifted their cards at the corner and placed some chips in the centre of the table, matching each other's bids.

"I'll take another," Wes said.

"Yep, I'll take another one, too," the stocky man said, his smile wider than the Bristol Channel.

Again, the croupier turned over a card in front of each man. Wes received an eight of diamonds, and the stout man was dealt a ten of spades.

"Hey, what's going on here? I saw the look between you two. I'm not happy about this. Get the manager."

"Wow, nothing like dealing with a sore loser," Wes told the man.

"Sore loser my arse. I'm on a winning streak—at least I was until you started making eyes at this wench."

The croupier's mouth dropped open, and a few muscle-bound heavies approached the table as the crowd grew thicker.

Sensing there was trouble brewing, Kayli sought out Dave in the hordes of people circulating the area and motioned for him to get closer. He moved to within inches of Wes, and it was then that the croupier appeared to spot him. She leaned forward and whispered something in Wes's ear. That only angered the stocky man more.

The man flew out of his chair and pointed at the pair of them. "You see that, everyone? Tell me I'm wrong about thinking something is going on between these two. I demand to see the manager right away."

"Sit down, big man. She's done nothing wrong. It's you overreacting," Wes said. His gaze turned over his shoulder, and he said to Dave, "And what's your problem, mate? I know you, don't I?"

Dave shrugged and grinned. "Maybe I've just got one of those faces that always looks familiar in a crowd."

"Huh…maybe it's one of those faces that people are tempted to bop on the nose," Wes sneered back as he rose to his feet.

One of the heavies surged forward, knocking Dave out of the way in his haste to keep Wes seated at the table.

"Get your hands off me, you moron," Wes complained, his arms flailing.

Dave glanced across the room at Kayli. She motioned with her head for him to step back, out of harm's way. Dave disappeared into the crowd of nosey parkers, all eagerly anticipating a fight. With Dave a safe distance away, Kayli returned her attention to Wes—right as he spotted her in the crowd. Recognition sparked in his eyes, and he glared at her. Kayli smiled and tipped an imaginary hat at him. The colour in his cheeks rose, and Kayli wondered if that was through anger or embarrassment. He tried to get out of his chair, but the heavy standing behind him clamped a hand on his shoulder, forcing him to remain seated as a man in a tuxedo appeared alongside the croupier.

"What's going on here?" the man in the tuxedo demanded with authority.

"These two are up to something. I was racking up the money until she dealt him a good hand," the stocky man complained, jabbing his finger at the croupier.

"Is this true?" the man asked the blonde.

"No, sir. All I did was deal out the cards."

The manager turned his attention to the stocky man and smiled. "My staff are trustworthy, sir. I don't take kindly to false accusations in my establishment. Take your money and leave now."

"What? You can't do that! I have the right to spend my money how I want to. She's at fault here. You should be sacking her and dealing with this piece of shit," he said, pointing at Wes. "Not kicking me out."

"Mr. Porter has been coming here for years, and we've never had any problems with him. I object to customers questioning the morals of my staff. You've made yourself perfectly clear. Therefore, I'm requesting that you quietly leave my establishment of your own free will. Or do you insist on doing things the hard way? It might mean that you end up with yet more egg on your face if my guys have to escort you off the premises, but the choice is yours, sir. I run a tight ship here and have never had any of my girls accused of favouring a customer before. I've taken that as a personal insult."

The stocky man's shoulders dipped in defeat as he got to his feet. "I can see it's going to be a waste of time and energy on my part arguing the toss with you. If you don't want my cash, there are plenty of other casinos in the area who would snap my hand off. I'm a very wealthy man."

The manager nodded once and, with a broad smile, bid the man goodbye. He clicked his fingers, summoning up two of his goons. "Escort the gentleman off the premises, will you, lads? Right, folks, the show is over. Get back to winning your fortune and having a good time."

The mingling crowd dispersed, murmuring their dissatisfaction as the stocky man was removed from the room. Kayli watched the proceedings intently. The manager leaned over and whispered something in Wes's ear, smiled at the croupier, then worked his way through the thinning crowd. The heavy behind Wes yanked him to his feet and forced Wes to follow the manager. Kayli picked out Dave in the crowd and gestured for him to go after them. She did the same until a goon spotted her and marched towards her.

"Going somewhere, little lady?"

"To the ladies'. Is that allowed?"

"The toilets are that way." He spun her around and pushed her gently towards the exit.

"All right. There's no need to be so heavy-handed."

The goon's breath ghosted close to her ear. "You think that's heavy-handed? Any more lip, and you'll be wishing you'd kept your mouth shut."

Seething, Kayli reached in her pocket and extracted her warrant card. She spun around and shoved it in the man's face. "You might want to reconsider the way you're talking to me, big man, or I'll take you down the station and throw you in a cell overnight on an assault charge."

The man's small eyes narrowed farther. "Whatever. I've asked you politely to leave, and you've refused. I think you'll find the law is on my side on this one, love." He pointed out several cameras around the room. "The proof is there for all to see."

Frustrated, Kayli stomped on the man's foot and legged it for the door. She knew the action was childish, but it was the only answer she could come up with at short notice and after a long day at work. When Dave joined her in the car park a few minutes later, she was still chuckling to herself.

"Are you asking for trouble? That goon could have put you in hospital."

"I know. The devil in me reared its head. Before I knew what was happening, it was too late to back down. Enough about that. Did you see where Wes and the manager went?"

"I got as close as I could without the heavies clocking me. They went into the manager's office. I get the impression the manager wasn't too happy about the incident disrupting the evening. What do you want to do now?"

"We need to hang around, see if he comes out soon and what state he's in. My take is the manager was livid and is going to punish him. How the hell did he have the money to play tonight if he's in that much debt? That's gonna tick the manager off, right? It should do."

"God knows where these gamblers get the money to feed their addiction. I'd be straight down the travel agent's if I had a few thousand going spare."

Kayli nodded. "Me, too. Come on, get in. I made us a flask of coffee."

They were halfway through their drink when Wes emerged from an alleyway alongside the casino. His face was beaten to a pulp. He staggered across the car park then fell into his car.

"Shit! He can't drive in that state," Kayli whispered as if the man was likely to hear her.

Dave pointed at the steps leading down from the casino. "Wait a minute. What's this?"

The blonde croupier ran across the car park and headed straight for Wes's car. She yanked open the driver's door, bent down, and smoothed a hand over Wes's hair, comforting him. After a few seconds of conversation, Wes got out of the car, walked around it, and slid into the passenger seat. The blonde jumped behind the steering wheel and started the engine.

Kayli opened her door, threw the remains of her coffee in the gutter, and gave her cup to Dave to hold while she switched on the engine and followed Wes's vehicle out onto the main road. Kayli let a few cars pass before she pulled out.

"Gonna take a bet where they end up?" Dave asked, finishing the last of his coffee and slipping the cups back into the carrier bag.

"I'm thinking at her place. I hope I'm wrong about that."

"Why?"

"If they go back there, that means that Cathy will be alone at the house, unless someone has stayed overnight with her. Irresponsible on his part if he hasn't arranged that."

"So what are we going to do if they end up back at hers?"

Kayli shrugged. "Not sure. Okay, do me favour. Ring the station and get a squad car to drive past his place, see if there's a car parked outside."

"Good thinking. On it now."

Kayli continued to follow the vehicle through the town, which was lit up in all its glory, while Dave rang the station. He made the arrangements then ended the call as Wes's car came to a stop on Harrington Road outside a small house. Kayli parked up in a free space and strained her neck to see what the couple did next. The blonde hopped out of the car and rushed around to the passenger side. She helped Wes out of the seat and through the gate. She propped him up against the wall while she inserted her key into the lock then helped him inside.

Dave's mobile rang. "Yep. That's great. Thanks, Sergeant." He turned to Kayli. "Apparently, there is a car outside Porter's home."

Kayli exhaled a large breath. "Phew! That's a relief. Not sure how we would have got around that, apart from spending the night watching over Wes's house."

"Really? It would have come down to that? So, what now?"

"Yep. I'm an idiot. I know. Hmm… What's the likelihood of him leaving here before dawn breaks?"

"None. What are you saying, that we should call it a day and go home? Because I'd jump at the chance."

"Might as well call it a night. I'd rather not sit around here, imagining what they're going to get up to."

"I'm with you on that one."

Kayli headed back to the casino, where she dropped Dave off at his car. Still wide awake and feeling at a loose end, she drove through the town again and parked the car close to the nightclub where Mark worked. He was standing outside the club, talking to another doorman. She exited the vehicle and crossed the street, but she halted when a group of girls approached the club and began flirting with the doormen. A few of the girls even took the liberty of grabbing a selfie with Mark and the other man. Seething, annoyed that she had gone out of her way to drop by and see her husband, Kayli ran back to the car and screeched away from the scene.

Sleep evaded her until Mark walked in the house at three-thirty. He crept into the bedroom, and she heard him undress and visit the bathroom before he slipped into the bed beside her.

"I'm awake," she said.

He snuggled up behind her. She tensed up. She couldn't help it as the images of him and the girls flickered through her mind.

"Hey, what's wrong, baby?" He kissed her neck.

Kayli chastised herself. She knew she was being foolish, possibly even childish. *Is this why he hasn't been desperate to find a new job? How often does that kind of thing happen to him? Does he enjoy the adoration these sluts fling at him?* She couldn't let him know what she'd seen. "I'm frustrated because I've been trying to sleep, and it's just not happening." She rolled over to face him as his arm slid across her flat tummy.

"Something bugging you?" he asked, snuggling into her neck.

"Not really. How was work?"

"The usual. Busy keeping out the riffraff and ensuring no troublemakers entered the club."

"Oh, right. Do you ever get any hassle from the girls? Anyone ever make a nuisance of themselves? When they're drunk perhaps?"

"Not really. Nothing more than usual anyway. Any specific reason you should ask?"

"Nope. Just making conversation. Thinking back to when I used to hang out at nightclubs, I know the girls were attracted to the doormen wearing their tuxes. I just wondered if that type of thing still went on."

"Occasionally. There's no need for you to be jealous, though, baby. It's you I come home to."

Kayli snorted. "I'm not jealous in the slightest. Actually, when I used to witness that kind of behaviour in my younger days, I always felt sorry for the girls fawning over the men like a bunch of saddos," she replied with more venom in her tone than she'd intended.

He kissed her on the lips, a gentle kiss that intensified. Glad that he couldn't see how upset she was, she gave in and returned the kiss as a single tear of frustration slipped down her cheek. The kiss inevitably led to more, and any fears she'd foolishly had of losing him were swiftly pushed aside.

CHAPTER ELEVEN

When Kayli arrived at work the following day, she called a meeting with the team first thing to go over what Dave and she had witnessed the evening before.

"We need to question him, don't we?" Dave asked.

"We do. I need to find something in particular to go on before I tackle him, though. I have a feeling he's going to be a wriggly worm to interview. Let's say I'm not feeling a hundred percent confident about confronting him just yet. So what else do we have?"

"Off the top of my head, the exes need to be tracked down and questioned, plus the ex-friend."

Kayli nodded. "I'm going to ring Amelia Watson now to see if she can tell me when the funeral is going to take place. I'm also thinking that we should go back to the croupier's house and question her about the relationship."

Dave shrugged. "Maybe. I don't think it's likely that you'll get anything out of her, but we can try. She wasn't that forthcoming when I spoke to her."

"Maybe that'll change after what we witnessed last night. We'll leave it an hour or so. Ten o'clock should be a reasonable time to pay her a visit. Hopefully, Wes will have left by then. I'll be in my den until then." She walked into her office then picked up the phone as soon as she sat down.

"Hello?"

"Amelia, sorry to trouble you. This is Kayli Bright, the SIO on your sister's case. We met the other day."

She gasped. "Oh, hello. Please tell me you've caught the murderer?"

"Sorry, no. Not wishing to raise your hopes, but we believe we're getting closer every day. I was calling to see if there had been any arrangements regarding the funeral? I'd like to attend to pay my respects."

"It's tomorrow. Wes was keen to have it quickly."

"Did he say why?"

"Not really. He said we all need to begin to heal after our loss. I agree with him to some extent, although I can't see me getting over Jess's death any time soon."

Kayli chewed on her lip for a second, repressing the urge to tell her where her brother-in-law had spent the night. "Maybe it's for the best. Where is the funeral being held?"

"All Saints church, do you know it?"

"I do. What time?"

"At eleven o'clock. I'm apprehensive about it. I've never had to say goodbye to someone so close to me. Not sure how I'm going to cope, if I'm honest."

"People will understand if they see you break down. Just be yourself and do what comes naturally. No one will expect you to be bright and breezy, I'm sure."

"Thank you. I'll take your advice on board. I guess I should go. Promised Mum I'd go round there to help her with the buffet for the wake. Mum insisted she should do it rather than spend thousands going to a venue."

"Mums are like that. Good luck, at least it will keep you all occupied today. I'll see you tomorrow."

"Thank you, Inspector."

Kayli ended the call with a heavy feeling in her heart. The thought of Wes in the arms of another woman so soon after his wife's death did little to alleviate her mood. She returned to the incident room to collect Dave. "Sod it. Dave, forget what I said about going round there at ten. We'll go now instead. I'm fed up with mollycoddling people. This is a murder enquiry, after all."

"I'm with you on that one. What if Romeo is still there?"

"We'll cross that bridge if and when we come to it. Let's get a move on."

~ ~ ~

They drew up outside the croupier's house, and Kayli let out a relieved sigh that Wes's car had gone. "That clears a path for us."

"I wonder if she's going to clam up and refuse to speak."

"Only one way to find out," Kayli replied, stepping out of the car.

They walked up the path, and Kayli rang the doorbell. She looked up. The bedroom curtain twitched. Kayli rang the bell a second time when it remained unanswered.

Finally, the blonde opened the door, wearing a skimpy nightie that left little to the imagination. Dave coughed a little to clear his throat, amusing Kayli.

"You two! What do you want from me, for fuck's sake?"

Kayli pushed past her and entered the hallway. "A minute of your time."

"You can't barge in here like that. I have rights. I know my rights."

"Funny that, so do we. Look, we can either do this the easy way or the hard way. The hard way would be hauling your arse down the station as you are. I'm sure the guys down there will enjoy the view."

Her mouth opened and closed for a few seconds before she huffed and slammed the front door shut behind Dave. She yanked on the hem of her nightie and marched ahead of them into the lounge, where she sat, her legs crossed at the ankles, her hands pulling the short garment down her thighs to hide her modesty again. "What's this about?"

"We'd like to ask you a few questions about your relationship with Wes Porter."

"I don't have to answer your questions."

"Oh yes, you do. We're conducting a murder enquiry. Now answer the question."

Her eyes watered up quickly, and her gaze dropped to the floor at Kayli's feet. "I've got nothing to tell you."

Kayli stood. "Cuff her as she is, Dave. We're taking her in."

Moira tucked her legs under her and reached for a cushion to place over her lap. "No, wait! Please, I don't want to go to the station. I've done nothing wrong."

Kayli sat again and glared at the woman. "Except sleep with a woman's husband behind her back. A woman who has since been murdered."

"I have nothing to do with that. I didn't know he was married, not to begin with."

"How long?"

"Six months, give or take a few days."

"When did he reveal he was married?" Kayli pressed, angry at the woman on Jess's behalf.

"After three months. He treated me like a princess. Couldn't do enough for me in the beginning."

"Has your relationship changed in the past few months?"

"Yes, he's become distant since he told me the truth. You get that with some men. It's all a game to them until they're found out."

"This has happened to you before?"

"Yes. I don't want to be a man's bit on the side. Wes promised me the earth and more."

"How did you find out?"

"He let it slip one day about his daughter. When I questioned him about Cathy, he broke down and admitted that he was married."

"Why didn't you dump him when you found out about Jess?" Kayli asked, deliberately using the dead woman's name to twist the knife.

"I'm ashamed to say I was in too deep by then."

"Meaning what? That you'd fallen in love with him?"

"Yes. He's addictive. He knows how to treat me well."

"Okay, are you aware that he is saddled with a huge debt? You know, because of his gambling habit. You must be aware how much he spends at the establishment where you work, right?"

"He told me he'd come into a lot of money lately."

"Did he now? You see, that's where your little tale falls to shreds, Moira. Aren't you really with him because he's fond of splashing the cash on you?"

Her hand swept over her face and her cheeks deepened in colour. "No. I love him because of who he is and how he treats me."

"As a bit on the side? Don't you have any self-respect?" Kayli found it hard to contain the anger bubbling inside her. "What did he tell you about Jess? The usual tripe about my wife doesn't understand me? Am I correct?"

She inhaled a shuddering breath. "Yes. I'm sorry. I should have listened to my head instead of my heart. It's too late now."

"Too late? Oh, I see you're referring to Jess's death. Tell me, haven't you ever wondered about that?"

Her brow wrinkled and she chewed her lip. "People have accidents all the time."

"Okay, I think you missed something at the beginning of our conversation. I distinctly remember telling you that we're conducting a murder enquiry, or did you choose to ignore that statement on purpose? Perhaps you and Wes are in cahoots. You planned her murder between you. Tell me, have you ever been to Hawthorn Stables?"

"No. Why would I be seen dead at a stable?" She had the decency to flinch when she uttered the word *dead*.

"You seriously expect me to believe you?"

She threw the cushion aside and leapt to her feet, obviously forgetting how she was dressed. "Believe what you like. I know my rights. I'm entitled to be questioned with a solicitor present."

"I'm wondering how you're so well versed in your rights, Moira."

"I'm not. Common sense tells me that you can't come barging in here, trying to trip me up. I'm guilty of nothing except loving Wes Porter. Throw me in prison for that if it is indeed a crime."

"It's a crime if you're perceived to have been having an affair at the time of Jess's death. What do you know about her death?"

"Nothing. I was told that she'd had an accident. This is the first I've heard that you believe she was murdered. I swear, I have nothing to do with this."

"Pillow talk! Don't you and Wes ever confide in each other while you're in bed together?"

"No. We're otherwise occupied."

"Ahh, such as last night, for instance?"

She fell into her chair again and stretched her nightie down the length of her slim thighs. "Yes."

"Even though he was battered to a pulp? Didn't you ask yourself why he was beaten up by your workmates?"

"No. I never asked."

"I'm no Einstein, but even I find it hard to fathom why a person having a word with your manager would end up taking a major thrashing—or is that a regular occurrence at the casino?"

"Of course it isn't. He told me it was because he'd been cheeky in my boss's office. I took him at his word."

"The truth is I think your boss has come to the end of his tether, what with your boyfriend owing him over fifty grand."

Her eyes bulged. "What? I don't believe you. Wes would have told me if he was in debt. He loves me."

"I doubt that. Wes is selfish beyond words. The inheritance he spoke about was *his wife's* inheritance, not his. He's penniless...do you still love him?"

"Yes. Until I hear all this from his mouth. I don't believe a word you're telling me."

"Then you're more foolish than I first thought. I think you should get dressed and come with us." Kayli saw Dave look her way out of her peripheral vision.

"Why? I haven't done anything wrong. Please, don't make me come with you," she pleaded as the tears cascaded down her cheek.

"You'll be assisting us with our enquiries. I feel you're holding back, not telling us everything you know."

"I'm not. I swear I'm not. I've done nothing wrong. I'm a normal working-class girl."

"Who works in a casino. There's nothing wrong in that, unless you believe the man who confronted you and Wes last night. Did you cheat?"

"No. It's called gambling. Nothing is written in stone at that place. One hand, you win; the next, you lose."

"Okay. But you're also guilty of having an affair with a man whose wife has been murdered. Are you still telling me that I'm wrong to take you in for further questioning?"

"Yes. Please, you've got this all wrong."

"Then I'll do a deal with you. You tell me what you know about Jess's death and promise me that you won't go running to tell Wes about the conversation we've had this morning, and I promise not to take things further."

Surprised, she shook her head. "Please, you have to believe me when I say I don't know anything about her death. He told me she died in a horse-riding accident. I won't say anything to him because after today, I want nothing more to do with him, especially if you're telling me he killed her."

"I never said that. However, the evidence we have uncovered so far certainly points in his direction. I think you're wise to end things with him. To me, he seems a devious man riddled in debt. Not sure why anyone would want to be involved with anyone like that, no matter how silver-tongued he is."

"I agree. I'm sorry his wife died the way she did. I genuinely didn't know he was married or he had kids in the beginning. I would never have become involved if I had."

"I believe you. So there's nothing more you can tell us about Jess?"

"No. He rarely spoke about her when he was with me." Her gaze dropped to the floor, and she fidgeted in her seat. "We were too busy doing other things."

"I can imagine. All right, I'm going to leave you my card. If you think of anything that might be useful to our investigation in the meantime, will you give me a call?" Kayli crossed the room and handed her the card.

"Of course I will. I never signed up for any trouble. I do all I can to avoid it wherever possible. I promise you there was nothing going on at the casino. That man was wrong. All Wes was guilty of in that instance was flirting with me. That man read the situation wrong."

Kayli believed the young woman and smiled. "We'll leave things there for now. Thank you for seeing us."

"Can you show yourselves out?"

"Of course." Kayli and Dave left the room.

Dave whispered, "Are you going to trust her?"

Kayli raised a finger, urging him to remain quiet until they were out of the house. She closed the front door behind them. "I've got little option but to believe her at this stage. Maybe it's a woman thing, but I believe her. She looked shocked by the whole situation. I truly don't think it was all about the sex in her case. All she's guilty of is falling in love with Wes. Now that she's seen him in a different light, that will signify the end of their relationship. At least it should do."

Before getting in the car, Kayli glanced back at the house. Moira looked out the bedroom window, and Kayli hoped she wasn't wrong about the woman. Otherwise, that could have a devastating effect on the case. Only time would tell. However, her instinct was telling her she was right.

"Where are we going now?" Dave asked once they were in the car.

"We need to visit the rest of the people on our list. Let's see if we can do that today before we attend the funeral tomorrow."

"Great, that's something to look forward to—not," Dave complained, watching the fields go past the side window.

"You know what it's like at funerals. Some can be fraught affairs where people tend to drop their guard. Let's hope this one turns out to be like that."

"Clutching at straws comes to mind. I say we should bloody pull Wes Porter in and interview him at the station. I guarantee that'll shake him up."

"I'm conscious that he has a vulnerable sixteen-year-old daughter at home."

"Ha! *You* might be. Shame he didn't think about her last night when he was banging Moira back there."

Kayli tutted. "You have a terrible way with words sometimes. Leave the woman alone."

"Whatever," he replied immaturely.

They spent the rest of the day chasing their tails. Every person they set out to track down proved to be elusive. No one was at home, and not one of the neighbours knew where that specific person could be found. Frustrated, Kayli told the team to go home and to reconvene bright and early at eight o'clock the next morning. Before leaving the station, she reminded Dave to wear a black tie and suit for work the following day. Kayli also instructed Graeme to do the same in case she decided to take him to the funeral with them for added assistance.

She had a strange feeling deep in her gut that the funeral was going to be anything but a walk in the park.

CHAPTER TWELVE

The next morning, the weather turned out to be warm and pleasant, which was unusual, considering that they were gathering at a graveside. Every funeral Kayli had ever attended had been conducted in the rain. She arrived at the station at ten minutes to eight to find the ever-efficient Donna sitting at her desk, beavering away.

"You're keen, as usual. Have you been here long?" Kayli asked, heading straight for the vending machine.

"About ten minutes. Thought I'd make a start on things. What time are you setting off for the service today?"

"The funeral is at eleven, so we should leave here around ten-thirty. Coffee?"

"Thanks! That would be great. Are you expecting trouble today?"

Kayli returned to Donna's desk and placed a coffee in front of her. "Let's just say I'm erring on the side of caution and asking Graeme to come with us."

"Very wise. The family seem friendly enough, but I get a bad feeling about the husband, and I haven't even met the man."

"Maybe it's a woman thing? Dave sometimes has problems seeing the same thing as me in a suspect."

"You talking about me, boss?" Dave breezed into the room, along with Graeme.

"Nothing derogatory for a change," Kayli replied, rolling her eyes at Donna. "I'll be in my office if anyone needs me. Be ready to leave at ten-thirty, gents."

"What? So you want me to come with you?" Graeme asked.

"I get the feeling we're going to need an extra pair of hands today."

"You and your bloody gut feelings," Dave grumbled under his breath just loud enough for her to hear.

"I know you're envious, Dave, but try and keep it in check for now." Kayli winked at the sniggering Donna then disappeared into her office.

She finished her coffee then dived into the mound of brown envelopes sitting on her desk. At ten o'clock, Dave entered the room with a fresh cup of coffee in his hand. "Thought you'd want another caffeine fix before we leave."

"Thanks, I appreciate that, Dave. Can't say I'm looking forward to today."

"What's there to look forward to? Seeing a lot of people in tears wiping the snot from their noses?"

"Do you have to be so crude?"

He shrugged. "It's the truth. Want to go in two cars, or shall the three of us pile into yours?"

"Ask Graeme if he's willing to take his car. It's pretty local, so he won't use much petrol. I should be finished with this crap in fifteen minutes, give or take."

"Okay, we're ready when you are. Do we need to run through what's expected of us today, or are we going to wing it when we're there?"

"Tell you what you can do in readiness for the off—ensure your phone is fully charged and ask Graeme to do the same."

"Any specific reason?"

"I want to film people, discreetly, of course, gauge their reactions to the other mourners. You know what it's like at funerals. People's raw feelings are on show. That's why I like to attend them whenever possible."

"I'm with you. I'll let you get on."

~ ~ ~

Fifteen minutes later, Kayli walked back into the incident room. "Are we ready to go?"

Dave and Graeme unplugged their phones from their chargers and checked them. "I'm at eighty percent charge. What about you, Graeme?"

"Ninety percent. I'll put it on save-battery mode. It'll help if I have to take any videos."

"Good thinking, Graeme," Kayli replied. "Let's go. We'll keep in touch, Donna."

"I'm tempted to say have a good time but I don't suppose you will in the circumstances, boss." Donna twisted her mouth and smiled.

"Can't say I'm looking forward to it. See you later."

The three of them left the office and marched through the corridor and down the stairs as if they were on a mission. Graeme jumped in his car and followed Kayli and Dave to the church, which was located a few miles away.

Kayli pulled into the car park and was surprised at how many vehicles were already there. "Hmm…considering how many cars are here, this might prove to be more interesting than we first suspected."

Graeme joined them, and the three of them walked towards the entrance of the church. "You two stay here. I want to pay my respects to Jess's family. Keep your eyes peeled." Kayli made a beeline for Amelia Watson.

Amelia saw Kayli heading her way and spoke to the couple she was standing with. The couple drifted away. Amelia shook Kayli's outstretched hand. "Hello, Inspector. It's so nice of you to attend. Mum and Dad will be pleased to see you."

"How are you all holding up?"

"Mum's very tearful today. Dad's taken her to the loo across the road at the pub. I'm not sure how she's going to cope when she sees the coffin. I'm dreading seeing it myself. We went to see Jess yesterday at the undertaker's, and it was extremely tough on all of us. Not sure Mum slept very well last night."

"It's a really difficult situation for parents to come to terms with when they lose a child, no matter what age the child is."

"I think you're spot-on. No one should outlive their children. That's all Mum keeps saying, and she's right, of course. Any news for us?"

"Not yet. We're having trouble locating the list of people you supplied me with. I don't suppose any of them are here, are they?"

"Some of them will be, all except Deanne Mitchell. I didn't see the fun in sending an invite to her."

"Interesting. Maybe I could ask you to point the ex-boyfriends out to me later, if that's all right?"

"I'd be happy to. There's one of them now. Stuart Collins." She nodded at a man standing alongside a woman dressed in black wearing a large hat and high heels.

"Thanks, that helps. I'll try and have a word with him after the service. Not sure there's enough time now. Anyone else?"

Amelia scanned the nearby crowd. Her gaze settled on Wes and Cathy on the far side of the gathering before she continued to scan the rest of the mourners. "I can't see anyone else. Maybe they couldn't make it. Not everyone responded to the note I sent them. Ah, here's Mum and Dad now."

Kayli turned to see a distraught-looking Mary Watson clinging on to her bewildered husband's arm. She smiled at them, hoping to put them both at ease a little. "Sorry to meet again under such circumstances. How are you both?"

"'Surviving' is the best way to describe it, Inspector. Have you caught the person responsible yet?" Gerald Watson asked, tears welling up in his grey eyes.

"Unfortunately not. We're still sifting through all the evidence. Hopefully, we'll be able to put all the pieces together soon."

"Shouldn't you be out there instead of hanging around here, in that case?"

"Gerald, please. I don't want any unpleasantness. Not today," Mary chastised her husband.

"Dad, be fair. Don't go blaming the inspector when she's been kind enough to come here today."

"I apologise. Please forgive my rudeness, Inspector. I know you're doing your best."

"I appreciate how frustrating this must be for you all. Please, I want you to be assured that we're doing everything we can to find this person. I wanted to take time out to show my respects to your daughter."

"We appreciate that," Mary said.

The crowd shuffled back to allow the hearse entry to pull up outside the church. Amelia wrapped her arm around her mother's shoulders when she started to sob. Gerald stood on the other side of his wife, holding her hand firmly.

The coffin was decked in beautiful wreaths. One said 'daughter', another 'wife', and the final one 'mother'.

Tears prickled as the emotions emanated surrounding Kayli. "I'll leave you to it. I'll be thinking of you all during the service."

Amelia smiled. "Thank you," she said, her voice catching.

Kayli wandered back to Dave and Graeme as the mourners filed into the church. "I think this is going to be tougher than I anticipated." She dabbed her eyes with a hanky.

"You're a daft mare at times," Dave said, elbowing her in the ribs.

"It shows I care, Dave. Have you spotted anything unusual in my absence?"

Both men shook their heads and Dave replied, "Nope, nothing out of the ordinary. Did Amelia give any pointers as to who was here?"

"Yep. I've clocked Stuart Collins so far. He's here with a woman. That's all she managed to point out before her parents arrived. Let's take our seats at the back of the church and keep an eye on things from there."

Wes walked into the church alongside Cathy, deposited her in the front pew next to Amelia and Mary Watson, then left the church again. For an instant, his gaze met Kayli's. He dipped his head to avoid further eye contact with her. Kayli was appalled by the bruises and split lip he was sporting and recognised how difficult it must have been for a man to disguise such a battering.

Moments later, the organist started playing Elton John's *Candle in the Wind* to accompany the pallbearers carrying the coffin into the church. Wes and Gerald were amongst the six men who carried the casket up the aisle to its resting place on the large stone plinth.

The six men then dispersed and took their seats. The service was read by a priest in his sixties, who had a kind face and wore spectacles perched on the end of his nose. A few friends read their eulogies aloud before Wes stood to read his. To Kayli's ears, his words sounded cheap and insincere, as though they'd been extracted from either a book or downloaded from the internet. He kept his head down as he read, not once taking the time to survey the mourning crowd in front of him. Kayli reprimanded herself for thinking badly of the man. Maybe he was the type who struggled to handle grief. Then a little voice reminded her what the man had been up to in recent months behind his wife's back. She narrowed her eyes as she focused, trying to use her womanly powers to read what was really going on in his head.

After he'd concluded, Wes returned to his seat next to Cathy, who was in tears. He threw an arm around her neck, and she buried her head in his chest, continuing to sob openly. Once the service had finished, the crowd left the church and followed the priest to the burial plot. Kayli, Dave, and Graeme began the task of casting their eyes over the mourners. Kayli spotted Cordelia Porter standing alongside a tall teenager, presumably her son, Patrick. She wracked her brain, but she was certain she hadn't seen them inside the church. Cordelia spotted Kayli and smiled. Kayli returned the smile but then shifted her gaze to Patrick. His head was down. Every now and then, he glanced up, mainly to stare in his father's direction before his head dropped again. Something in the boy's eyes when he stared at his father was unnerving.

She leaned over and whispered to Dave, "Watch the tall lad at the front."

"Who is he?"

"Wes's son. Can you move over there, try and film him?"

Dave nodded and drifted away. "Graeme, can you start filming the mourners as discretely as possible for me?"

"Sure. I'll step back and do it from behind a tree over there."

"Perfect. I'm not sure what I'm looking for, so just film everyone."

Graeme stepped away from her. Kayli kept her gaze on the young man. At one point, she shifted it to Cordelia. Sweat developed on the woman's top lip, and she wiped it away several times. The woman seemed agitated. *What's going on, Cordelia? What are you giving away?*

Kayli decided to move closer to the woman and her son. She placed herself behind Amelia and her parents and watched the proceedings from there. Cordelia seemed panic-stricken and she searched the crowd for Kayli.

Her son looked up at his father with what could only be described as venom in his eyes. The boy matched his mother's agitation. *What the hell is going on here? Is Patrick angry with his father about something? Why show his anger here?* Kayli had the feeling that something was about to kick off. She scanned the crowd for Dave and Graeme, regretting her decision to send them off in different directions. She had to get nearer to Cordelia and her son.

The priest drew everyone's attention and the final people shuffled into position at the graveside. He conducted the burial service then invited the family members to say a few words and throw a handful of dirt on the coffin. Wes encouraged Amelia and her mother and father to go first.

A lump appeared in Kayli's throat when she listened to them say their farewells, but her gaze remained fixed on Cordelia and her son. His chin was still on his chest, and his hands clenched together in front of him. Cordelia kept looking at her son's face and even leaned over to whisper in his ear once. He didn't react in the slightest.

Wes and Cathy approached the graveside together, then each of them picked up a handful of dirt.

Holding a white rose in her hand, Cathy scattered the dirt and let go of the beautiful flower. "I love you, Mum. I'll miss you every day until we meet again. I'll never forget you."

At Cathy's words, Patrick closed his eyes and shook his head briefly. Kayli wondered if the half-siblings were close.

The last person to bid Jess farewell was Wes. He removed a large handful of dirt from the wooden box, carved out the sign of the cross over his chest, and threw a single-stemmed white lily onto the coffin along with the dirt. "My love, I will never forget the joy you brought into our lives. Thank you for giving me such a beautiful daughter. I hope she turns out to be half the woman you were. I will never love someone as much as I loved you."

Kayli watched Cordelia's and Patrick's reactions. Patrick's mouth twisted, his hands clasped tighter together, and his head slowly rose to look at his father. His jaw clenched, and his eyes turned into slits. Patrick marched towards his father.

"Patrick, no! Don't do this," Cordelia shouted. "Not here, son. Not now."

Patrick was determined in his actions, and no one was going to stop him. Kayli shot a glance left then right, trying to locate her colleagues. Dave was staring right at her, while Graeme had his phone in position, filming what was emerging. It was clear they both sensed something major was about to kick off, too. Kayli motioned with her head for Dave to move with her. Together, they approached the father and son and the distance between them decreased.

"You did this… You're guilty of this. Call yourself a father? You *disgust* me. You deserted me as a boy to create your new family…" Patrick words grew louder, angrier.

Wes looked to Cordelia for help, but after her initial attempt to try to get her son to remain with her, she stayed still as if she'd sprouted roots.

"What are you talking about, boy?" Wes demanded, placing an arm in front of Cathy, who then took a step sideways to hide behind her father's back.

"She always got your attention…that bitch behind you. The day she was born was the day you lost interest in me, wasn't it?"

Wes's gaze scanned the bewildered crowd of mourners. "You're being ridiculous. I've always treated you and Cathy the same."

A demented laugh escaped Patrick's mouth. He marched faster towards his father, who was trying to back away from his raging son. Cathy screamed.

"Shut up, bitch, or I'll kill you like your mother. You're two of a kind anyway. You're both better off dead."

Kayli rushed past Wes and stood between him and his son. Dave grabbed Patrick's arm, preventing him from reaching his father.

"What do you mean, Patrick?" Kayli asked.

It was as if he didn't see them when Dave or Kayli planted themselves in his path. "They took everything from me. Mum has struggled to bring me up over the years because you were often too tight to part with your cash. Mum had to go back to work early because you refused to make the maintenance payments. You were keen to produce me. Not so keen on taking care of me financially, though. Not once that bitch came onto the scene."

"That's not true, Patrick. I love you. I've always done my best to care for you financially." Wes swallowed noisily.

Kayli knew immediately he was telling lies.

"Mum's pleaded with you recently to give us money for uni. She's been saving like mad for years to put me through college on her own because you don't give a shit. You had your own little tribe to be concerned about. Even though Jess inherited that money, none of it came our way."

"You're being ridiculous, son. That wasn't my money to play with. Jess always treated you well. Are you telling me that you did this? You killed my beautiful wife? Why? Why would you do such a twisted thing?"

Patrick's fingers contracted and released, and his chest inflated and deflated rapidly as his lip curled and his eyes glistened with anger.

Looking right through him, Kayli could tell his soul was tormented. "Patrick, we're going to ask you to accompany us to the station now."

His gaze left his father and slowly fell upon her. "She deserved it. You can't even comprehend to understand what it was like to be cast aside when that bitch came into the world. All my life, I've been treated as a second-class citizen by them. Not once have I ever been invited to their house. My mother has been a father and mother to me all my life because this waste of space didn't have the balls to go against his new wife's wishes."

"That's not true. My mother always tried to include you in our lives," Cathy shouted. "Dad, why is he telling all these lies?"

Patrick glared at his father again. "Go on, *Dad*. Tell her that I'm not lying."

Wes's shoulders dipped. "I thought it was for the best. It was my fault you never came to the house. Cathy is right—Jess wanted to do right by you, wanted to include you in our lives. It was me who let you down. I should be the one in that grave, not her. How could you kill her like that? What possessed you to go that far?"

For the first time, Patrick appeared to be taking his father's words on board. He ran a hand through his spiky hair, his expression changing from anger to confusion in a flash.

"Okay, that's it. We need to take you down the station now, Patrick." Kayli leaned around the troubled young man and gestured for Cordelia to join them. "I'll need you to come with him. He's a minor and will be treated as such."

Cordelia walked up to her son and placed an arm around his waist. "Why didn't you tell me you felt this way, love? What have you done?"

He collapsed into her arms at the magnitude of her words His legs gave way, and he dragged his mother down to the ground with him. She hugged him and rocked him back and forth as tears cascaded down her cheeks.

"Persuade everyone to go now, Dave, will you? Ask Graeme to help."

"Okay, boss. Have you got your cuffs on you?"

"I have. I don't think I'll be needing them, though, do you?"

Dave nodded and went in search of Graeme. They ushered the crowd away from the graveside. Off to her left, she listened to Amelia trying to explain to her confused parents what was going on.

Wes tapped her on the shoulder. "What happens now? He didn't mean to do it. I'm sure it wasn't his intention to kill her."

"That might be the case, but he did. He'll be placed in custody and will have to go through the system. Why don't you take Cathy home? It's been a traumatic day for her."

He wrapped an arm around his daughter's shoulder and led her away.

With one eye on Patrick and his mother, who were both sobbing, Kayli stepped towards Amelia and her parents. "I had no idea it would be Patrick. Sorry you and your parents had to deal with this."

"Did you know something like this would happen here today? Is that why you wanted to come?" Amelia asked, coughing to clear her throat.

"We tend to find some suspects can't handle the guilt at the graveside. I never expected this. Have you had much contact with Patrick over the years?"

"No. No contact at all with him. I remember seeing him once when he was a toddler, but this is the first time I've seen him since then. I'm shocked that he would hate Jess so much."

"I honestly don't think he did. He struck out at her because of his father's failings. He presumed that Jess was behind his father's absence over the years. He gravely misread the situation and now he'll be punished for his actions."

"Will the court be lenient on him, given the circumstances?" Amelia asked, not an ounce of anger showing on her face.

"Would you want them to be?"

"I don't know. It seems a shame—he has his whole life ahead of him."

Kayli rubbed the top of Amelia's arm. "You're a very compassionate lady."

Amelia shrugged. "He's family, sort of."

"I'll be in touch." Kayli returned to where Cordelia and Patrick were hugging each other on the ground, and the priest joined her.

He made the sign of the cross over the pair and said, "May the Lord have mercy on your soul."

Cordelia looked up at the priest and smiled. "Thank you, Father."

The priest gave a brief nod and backed away just as Dave and Graeme joined them.

"Come on, Patrick. Let's get you up on your feet and in the car," Dave said, hooking an arm through the young man's.

Patrick hugged his mother one last time then rose to his feet. Dave and Graeme accompanied him to the car.

Kayli helped Cordelia to her feet. "Are you all right?"

"Not really. I didn't have a clue. He's been so wrapped up in himself for years. I've read articles about kids coming from broken homes and thought his behaviour was normal. I've done my very best for him over the years, but it clearly wasn't good enough."

"Please, Cordelia, you mustn't blame yourself. It takes a lot to turn someone into a killer."

"Oh God, I'm going to have to live with that stigma for the rest of my life. I should have got him therapy, counselling of some kind. Poor Jess, none of this was her fault. She didn't deserve to die."

"I know. It's too late to start blaming yourself now."

"Will he go to prison?"

"Yes, not a full prison, but one where young offenders are placed. I'm sorry."

"Why did he do this? It's my fault. I should have realised he had a problem and obtained the right help."

"No one truly knows what goes on in the minds of our nearest and dearest."

Kayli walked Cordelia back to the car. She sat in the back seat with Patrick while Kayli and Dave sat in the front.

EPILOGUE

The interview proved to be one of the most satisfying and heart-breaking ones Kayli had ever endured. The duty solicitor turned up within ten minutes of Dave making the call. Cordelia was present but said nothing. She appeared to be too stunned to utter a word.

Patrick didn't hold back—years' worth of pent-up emotions tumbled out of his mouth. His words were full of regret and remorse. By the end of the interview, Kayli found herself feeling sorry for the teenager in spite of his callous actions. It was obvious that he'd intended only to cause an accident, not actually kill Jessica Porter. Kayli suspected the youngster would regret his decision for years to come.

Once Patrick had given his statement, he was placed in a cell to await transfer to a remand centre. He would then likely be transferred to the Young Offender Institution at Aylesbury. When they were alone, Cordelia broke down in Kayli's arms and sobbed. She was inconsolable for half an hour or more. Kayli's heart bled for the woman whose life had been turned upside down because of her son's spiteful act of petulance. Eventually, Cordelia pulled herself together enough to venture home. Kayli arranged with the desk sergeant for a squad car to give her a lift back to the church to retrieve her car.

When Kayli returned to the incident room, the team weren't as jubilant as they usually were at the end of a case. If anything, they were rather subdued.

Kayli left the station at just gone six and arrived home to find Mark in the kitchen, as usual, slaving away at the stove, rustling up pork chops, green beans, broccoli, and sautéed potatoes. She slid her arms around him.

"Hello, you. Have you had a good day at work?" He turned to face her.

"Not really. I don't want to talk about work. I want to talk about us. What we've become."

Mark frowned and held her at arm's length. "I wasn't aware that there was a problem between us, love."

"Maybe it's just me then. Something is screwing with my head, Mark, and I need to get it out. Please, don't judge me until you've heard everything I have to say. Promise?"

He switched off the gas under all the pots, and they sat at the table, their hands grasping each other's.

Kayli sighed. "To be honest with you, I'm not sure how much longer I can cope with our situation. I miss you when you're not around. I know I probably see more of you than I ever did when you were in the army, but I accepted that for some reason. Perhaps it's the fact that you were in a different country and so far out of reach that it didn't matter. Having you working down the road and not spending time with you is killing me—us."

He fell back in his chair. "I know we've had our differences about my job lately but I didn't realise things had got so bad for you, Kayli."

"I came to see you the other night," she admitted quietly.

His brow furrowed again. "You did? When?"

"The night before last. Dave and I were on surveillance and finished early after the suspect went home with a woman. As I was in town and at a loose end, I thought I'd drop by and say hello. I left my car and walked towards the nightclub just as a group of women appeared. They were fawning all over you, taking selfies and giggling. To my amazement, you did nothing to deter them. I drove home and spent the rest of the night tossing and turning."

"It happens, love. I know the group of girls you're referring to. One of the lasses in the group works as a barmaid at the club. That's the only reason Jeff and I allowed the selfies."

Mortified she'd read the situation wrongly, she dipped her head as shame rippled through her. "I'm sorry. I should have trusted you. It's been eating away at me ever since."

He left his chair and pulled her to her feet. His arms encircled her waist. "Kayli Bright-Wren, when are you going to get it through that head of yours that it's you I love? I might take a glancing look at other girls, but none of them would hold a torch to you. I know I keep saying this, but it's *you* I come home to every night. I've never, as far as I know, given you any reason to doubt my love for you, have I?"

She swallowed noisily as their gazes met. "No, I guess not."

"After all we've been through together, how could you doubt the love we share?"

"I wasn't."

His head inclined to the left. "I think your heart and your head are giving you mixed signals, love."

"I'm sorry, Mark. Sorry for doubting you. Will you ever be able to forgive me?"

"As daft as that question seems, of course I will, only if you promise me that if you have these feelings again you'll air them with me straight away. Don't let them fester."

"I promise."

"Right. Let me get the dinner out of the way, then we're going to spend the rest of the evening in bed, making up."

"What? But you have work."

He winked and kissed her gently on the lips. "I think it's about time I called in a sickie. You're worth it, Kayli. Worth risking everything for. You're my life, my soul, my everything. Please, please, don't ever forget that."

"I feel the same, and I won't, ever."

THE END

NOTE TO THE READER

Dear Reader,

Thank you for coming on the journey with me, did you guess who the killer was? More importantly did your heart go out to Jessica's family after all they had to endure?

Kayli and Mark will be featuring in a novella due out in October so stay tuned for that one.

Watch out for another cold case coming soon in the DI Sally Parker thriller series set in Norfolk, which is due to be released in September.

In case you haven't read the first book in the series here's the link.

https://melcomley.blogspot.com/p/wrong-place.html

As always, thank you for all your wonderful support. If you can find it in your heart to leave a review, I'd be eternally grateful.

Happy reading,
M A Comley

Made in the USA
Middletown, DE
16 September 2018